The Summer of Calamari

a novel

By

William D. Sullivan

1663 Liberty Drive, Suite 200
Bloomington, Indiana 47403
(800) 839-8640
www.AuthorHouse.com

This book is a work of fiction. People, places, events, and situations are the product of the author's imagination. Any resemblance to actual persons, living or dead, or historical events, is purely coincidental.

First published by AuthorHouse 05/20/05

ISBN: 1-4208-2266-7 (sc)

Library of Congress Control Number: 2005900369

Printed in the United States of America
Bloomington, Indiana

This book is printed on acid-free paper.

Cover art by D. Edward Ruffner

For my Mother

Book I
WALTER ROBERTS

Chapter 1
Brethren

It's never the right day to lose your childhood. Bicycle rides with bruised knees should last forever; the ice cream truck should follow us to purgatory; the tooth fairy should take dentures; and Santa Claus should always eat our cookies, but eventually we all lose the most sacred days of our lives. I remember tripping into what always seemed to be adulthood at age twelve. I guess average kids threw tantrums and rode in the "way back" of the family wagon at that age, but my life was a little different. My mother and I, on our own since my parents' divorce, stumbled along trying to do everything we could for each other, but there were only so many delicate hours she could spend with her child and still manage to put food on the table, and there is only so much psychological advice a twelve-year-old can give. Rather than worrying about bikes or skateboards, I turned my attention to what Mom would want for supper. I recall many hours spent comforting one another over TV dinners, but ultimately the two of us knew, like the chocolate pudding, we were not looking so good.

My unfortunate title for life is Leonard Harold Waldo Smith. My parents, who never managed to become any more original than their name suggests, dubbed me L.H.W. Smith for three reasons. According to family history, my mother loved the name Leo. Why? My father was always partial to Harold. Again, why? And they were both fans of Emerson. That, for me, always seemed to be the most amazing part. Why would two people who never managed to surface beyond the caste of middle class develop an addiction to Emerson? "Self-Reliance," "The Poet," and "Nature" were not inscribed on any bathroom wall I ever read, so I cannot imagine where my parents would have read him. Despite all odds, however, at some point in their meticulously average lives my parents read, and enjoyed, Ralph Waldo Emerson. I never witnessed either of them read anything he wrote, but then again why would they lie? It's like the man said, "Imitation is suicide." An occasional day passes when I do not wish he thought better of the middle name he would make famous, and published as Ralph Emerson, saving me the pain of Waldo, but here I am, Leo Smith.

I realize, of course, that my complaining about a name my parents loved is a little thankless, but you have to remember it's the negative that keeps us going. I am a firm believer if everything constantly remained positive, people would just sit down, take a deep, elongated breath, and stay there. "This is nice, Martha. Let's stay right here forever." That thought alone could turn a good meal bad. We can live through the negative because it is the sole reason we dig in, sweat, and grind to change the world. Nothing wrong with that.

The man who favored the name Harold lived a life a bit too clichéd to be favorably explained. However, without him my life would be a prologue, so I must recognize his part in my story. When thinking of him, I remember a time when things were better for our family, and a picket fence roamed within the realm of reality. My father worked on a small island in a Victorian hotel as a night watchman during the summers. I have scattered, fond memories of the years our family spent on the island, but they are only memories. "The Grand Hotel," in the town of New Shoreham, Rhode Island, otherwise known as Block Island, filled with affluent patrons from Memorial Day to Labor Day each summer. When the summer faded and the autumn months turned the cool, affable Atlantic into a forbidding foe, those patrons vanished, but my father remained as keeper of the hotel. We lived in a small but quaint (the word people kindly chose to call it) cottage behind the hotel. If nothing else, we relished one of the best ocean views on the island. My parents met on the island, married on the island, and years later returned to live on the island. What happened next was probably unavoidable, if you subscribe to fate.

I've never believed much in fate myself. It seems like such a strange idea that certain things are unavoidable. People have to decide for themselves whether to turn left or right at the end of a street, so if you get hit by a falling piano, you turned the wrong way, a life-threatening decision. Where is the fate in that? Rather than some cosmic phenomenon, fate always seemed like the last creation of a desperate person who ran out of excuses. Dodging bullets is a matter of speed; lifelong relationships are hard work; winning the lottery is luck. Fate?

One night, when my father leered into the dreary boredom of his illustrious, evening watch, something happened. It happened to me, it happened to my mother, my father, and even to some girl named Daisy Rae or Daisy Mae. I have forgotten her name, but I possessed the good fortune, even at that age, to be familiar with her type. She was an average "pack-for-a-week tourist," that is what the islanders called them, whose morals ran nearly as short as her cut off dungarees. On the night she came into my life my father decided he needed a change, my mother needed a sedative, and I needed answers. People often do not find what they need. What my parents got were lawyers. Richard Smith still works the night shift at the Grand Hotel in the town of New Shoreham on Block Island. Some people call him Dick.

My mother, Sarah Parsons, a name she immediately took back, was not cut from the breadwinners cloth. She never completed college lacking the money she needed to continue, and ended her formal education eight credits shy of an associate degree. Soon after dropping out, Sarah Parsons became Sarah Smith. Succumbing to the frustration of misspent years seeking higher education, Sarah found peace in the medium pace of waitressing on Block Island late in the spring of the year she wed. She found Richard almost as quickly as she found the island, and then left them in the same manner she came. More than anything else, Richard offered my mother a kind of direction she had never known in her confused young life. Like so many people, she clung to the life preserver because the ocean seemed too vast, an idea which only works if the preserver clings back. She fell in love with Richard and the island in a typical time of weakness, and left them both in her greatest moment of strength.

Since the divorce, my mother has become an unstable, but never too depressed, woman who spends countless moments of each day asking herself where she went wrong. Of course, I begin with a new answer every time, never aloud, always insightful. Sarah Parsons and I began forging our own road soon after Richard Smith began pushing up Daisy's.

That road led us to Ledyard, Connecticut, where my mother spent the first eighteen years of her life. In the Nutmeg State, she found comfort in the consoling thoughts of a few relatives, but readily accepted that we were on our own. The transition caused similar suffering to my mother and I, but she managed to make it more quickly and with less pain. Although her original state of disarray could be seen in the retreating background, her heart strengthened, removing doubt. One of the priceless lessons in life people seldom learn is the uselessness of doubt. Granted, if one decided to pole vault a burning building with a frozen rope, knowledge of the concept of doubt could become a necessary resource. However, if we can ignore those certain exceptions, doubt is rarely a constructive asset. A strong belief in your own self-reliance is the first powerful step in any direction. If you doubt, the journey lengthens. I don't think Sarah Parsons ever gave up on herself; she simply lost sight for a while.

I believe my mother's uncle on her mother's side managed to get her the secretarial job in the Human Resources Department of the local hospital. Work so often presents itself when a friend of the family, or your Uncle Vito, knows a guy who knows a guy who knows the woman who's in charge. Circles appear in nepotism, as well as history, and life itself. Propelled by newfound hope, Sarah even talked of returning to school, but could not find the time and eventually relinquished the idea. Nevertheless, she quickly planted her feet and supported herself again, leaving only her son to test his Emersonian reliance.

In the fall of my twelfth year, I prepared myself for change. If the leaves and the wind could adjust for change why should I fail? I spent the last few years of my life on an island where spotting three trees, in a one mile radius, meant you were in the woods. Comparatively, New England foliage was entertainment. I could stare through the trees and wonder curiously what went on in the darkness beyond. The wind burdened the branches, and leaves fell, but the shield of secrecy never really vanished. Even on a winter day, the pines filled in for those who couldn't cover their ground. They helped one another. It seemed like a nice idea.

Unfortunately, beautiful scenery failed miserably to offset the torment of starting over in a new school one year shy of my teens. My sixth grade class at the Block Island School consisted of three students, and although Ledyard could not be described as a boomtown at the time, it exposed a new world to me. That new world included multiple teachers and new middle school peers who came in all shapes and sizes. The latest of bloomers had not yet hit puberty, and the most advanced had already "done it." They were tall, short, fat, thin, pretty, handsome, and ugly, but they all shared one common character trait: None of them were particularly ambitious to meet the new kid

So it happened at the age of twelve that my true journey began. It began with no invocation to the muse, as I promised to serve as my own guide, my own inspiration. Actually, I promised myself I would avoid getting beaten up by the cool kids. Without alternatives, I quickly mastered the one skill that allowed me to believe in complete self-reliance. That one skill was naiveté. Waldo was loose.

The pain of a new place subsided each day from that very first when anonymity protected me well. The urban legend horror stories of being stuffed in a locker, or beaten by the school bullies never surfaced as reality and the true suffering existed only as one obvious, single emotion: loneliness. That feeling scattered for an immense day when I found myself, and my first real friend, on the playground of the Kennedy Middle School. Throughout the painful years of adolescence, this one particular day could be viewed only as the best of my young life, and as the years continue to fall on me like pianos on "ill-fated" men, those hours will be a few I will not forget. The two things that would keep me from all the misery of an ominous looking future were basketball and Walter Roberts.

During the December after my parents divorce, I rarely grappled with the solitude or the simple fact that I had not made any real friends. My worries pertaining to a surprise bathroom beating dissipated, and the possibility that cafeteria food was not that bad crept into my mind, but a Connecticut junior high school remained foreign territory in my sequestered life. Invisible in the classroom, hallways, and lunchroom, I wandered through each day wondering about the term "social life." The sun filled in as my best friend and I spent most of my afternoons with a basketball on the playground outside of the school. Those afternoons were governed by the New England weather, which allowed the temperature to drop thirty degrees in twenty-four hours. In fifty degree weather, I would spend two hours working on my jump shot, when it fell to twenty I spent two minutes. We only lived about three-quarters of a mile from the school allowing me to play until quarter past five, and still beat my mother home. Every day throughout the winter I lived alone on the courts, and I imagine many passing people questioned the intelligence of outdoor, winter basketball. I never seemed to get sick and if I played for more than those two minutes the chill of winter loosened its hold, defeated by the warmth of movement. Beating the cold required only my commitment. I glided through each day of school waiting like a weak-kneed contender for the last understanding bell to ring so I could gather my books, along with my weathered basketball, and attack the emptiness of the playground. I waited and lived from bell to bell. I waited alone.

As the snow melted and the weather warmed, a new face joined me on the playground each day after school. The two of us shared the four baskets, and occasional glances, without mixing words into the glory of anonymity. Day after day, we shared space without sharing ourselves. During those springing days, the playground felt most like the world I have come to know. The solitude I experienced on the courts throughout the winter should have been replaced with some sense of belonging. Instead, the loneliness became more obvious. I guess if you're completely alone you can rely on your own sense of solitude, Superman did it. The idea of existing alone isn't that scary, but realizing that you don't have to be alone and choosing it anyway, is the truly frightening end. The possibility of companionship just makes you realize what you're missing, and even Superman had Lois.

The four baskets on the playground became more neatly divided when basketball season ended for the school team, and my court became their court. The face and I remained in our own worlds and ignored the full court games now taking place everyday. We never tried to play and they never asked. The space between the last bell and the late bus became ours instead of mine and each day I silently begged them to go.

The typical pattern of the spring playground changed on that day, and I will never forget. Only three of the boys on the illustrious Kennedy team arrived at the playground that afternoon to bask in the glory of the sun and themselves. With full court games suspended for the day, they played a few games of "H-O-R-S-E" and "Twenty-one" until the first parent arrived to drag his child away from life, as he knew it. Complaining loudly, the boy was reluctantly shuttled off to the dentist or the doctor, wherever popular kids go when they are not busy hanging around being cool. Chris Dillinger, a starting forward for Kennedy, remained on the court with another boy who dribbled along as a "no-name" willing to live in the shadow of "the man." Confrontation hovered above the playground as the one thing the face and I both wanted to avoid, so it happened. "You guys want to play a little two on two," a midpubescent voice called over. I refused to acknowledge that Chris could have been talking to me so I just continued shooting.

"Hey, are you guys deaf or what?"

I knew I could no longer survive this encounter with denial so I thought quickly and saved myself by putting the cumbrous burden on the shoulders of "the face." "I'll play if he wants to." He would say no. He had no choice but to refuse knowing that they...

"I'll play." Without a bit of hesitation, he answered having no idea of the impending punishment we were bound to suffer. Maybe somewhere deep down I knew he could not refuse, but without hope what is a man, or a twelve-year-old boy. Among the caste system of the seventh grade it will always be better to lose than to "wimp out." Whether a fight, or gym class, or a basketball game, you couldn't back down, not for any reliable reason. He knew; he had to know.

From the base and the hypotenuse of the three-hoop triangle, the face and I walked toward the game of a lifetime. "Me and Billy against you guys. You can have the ball first."

I turned to "the face" that looked so intimidating until he offered a bright, white smile, which could have brought countries together. "My name's Walter. I think we're gonna get killed." He had wide, brown, friendly eyes, those big, white, perfect teeth, and dark skin. Really dark skin. That was my reaction.

"Leo."

"Take the ball out, Leo."

I passed the ball to Walter who quickly took one dribble to the right accelerating a step ahead of Billy. He then stopped short, raised the ball quickly, and elevated above his defender easily for an uncontested jump shot. He released the ball forcing it to sail toward the basket, and then over the basket and finally into the tennis courts behind the basket. "Sorry, man, my fault." Billy inbounded to Chris who took a couple of dribbles toward the baseline, stopped short, and shot over me. One-zero, two-zero, three, four.

"Leo, let's switch on defense." Walter could not contend for any prizes as the most accurate shooter in the game's history, but the kid could play defense. Four surprised boys watched Walter and I take a six to five lead as Chris Dillinger failed to score another basket. I scored all the points, and Walter played all the defense. Defending came naturally to him.

Just when Walter and I prepared to dribble into immortality, a car pulled into the parking lot and stopped twenty feet away from the basket. A very tall, attractive woman stepped out of the Honda and looked directly at Walter. The piercing tone of her voice nearly cracked the metal backboard. "Young man, I know there must be some reason why you're down here wasting your time when you should be home studying." At this point in life, the word studying had not yet entered into my limited vocabulary. Junior high students tackle the occasional science project, maybe even a weekly vocabulary test, but studying? Taboo. Walter threw an underhand pass to me and walked toward his books. Was there no justice? We were up six-five. Didn't she know that.

"How many times are we going to have this conversation, young man?" The kiss of death. She recited one of the questions all parents learn when they take "Classic Quotations 101." Walter made no motion to look at any of us, simply picking up his books and mumbling, "Gonna be here tomorrow?" I covered my mouth from her vision and responded quietly, "See ya tomorrow." A terrible day waits for every person who walks the globe, a day when you cease to remember what it means to be a child, what counts when you're young, and where the really meaningful lessons are taught. Maybe Walter would have skipped a couple pedantic problems on his math homework, but if we could have scored eleven points before they did, a small chunk of that fear of the powerful people who control the playground, and the world afterwards, is gone forever. I hate that fear. I still wonder if Walter knew it.

The friendship that began with a miraculous and eye-opening game of two-on-two matured daily under the nets of the playground. At least once a week Walter's mother would drive in, wrinkle her brow, and scold her son. "How many times are we going to have this conversation, young man?" I always wanted to sagaciously interrupt, "Once a week, Mrs. Roberts," but I never found the courage. I even started calling Walter "Week." He always thought I meant "weak," with regard to his jump shot, and I never told him otherwise. After all, his shot improved daily. Chris and Billy loved to tell the other guys the story about how Walter had been mercilessly summoned off the court, but I'm quite sure they always left out the score of the game when he walked toward the Honda.

Walter and I continued playing together, without any more challenges, as I'm sure none of the other pretentious players wanted to be the victims who lost to the kid who went home to mommy. Twelve –year olds, all twelve year olds can find an excuse for anything. We all wanted to protect our reputation, even those of us who did not really have one. No one could make fun of Walter for his mother's actions, because deep down they all knew he kept Chris Dillinger from scoring. That was colossal.

Walter Roberts soon became, and has always been, my best friend. One day during a stretch of about five—made—shots in a row, Walter stopped and looked at me in a way he never had before. His face filled with direction offering something more than concentration. "Why do you think those two black secret service agents were removed from their post across from the Memphis Hotel?" He was thirteen years old.

"What in the hell are you talking about, Week?" I assumed Walter entertained some random thought and would simply retract his question, but instead of firing away he held the ball in his relaxed arms and lowered his head. It seemed like the loose stones on the ground moved to avoid his glance. Neither praying nor crying, the curve of Walter's body and the shape of his frustration offered one of the saddest things I have ever seen. Years later, I understood the saddest thing about the day was that I really didn't know what he was talking about.

"I watched this show on TV last night with my mom and it said that Secret Service guys were moved from their post across from the Memphis Hotel on April 4,1968." Barely audible, his voice trembled.

"What happened on April 4,1968?"

He raised his head and trapped me in his glance. "That's the day Martin Luther King Jr. was shot." I wanted to just tell him I had no idea, or to stop talking and shoot the ball, but Walter's eyes and his tone convinced me to remain silent. He and I could be best friends, we could talk together, shoot together, and spend time together, but we could never create a perfect world. The barricades of society and the torments of history would never let us forget that Walter was black and I was white.

Finally Walter shot the ball and I released a silent breath to settle the tension I felt accompanying my ignorance. I knew in my heart that I still owed Walter some kind of answer. "I don't know, man. I don't know." My simple and useless answer allowed Walter to at least know I listened, and I think that picture alone illustrated what he wanted most.

"Yeah, I guess we'll never know." Walter took a final lay up before picking up his books and walking away from the playground. He took only a few steps before he turned around and looked back at me. We played for about two hours while the clouds of the afternoon sky dimmed the lights in ritual and the day looked more dusk. Walter's tall, thin frame cast no shadows. "You gonna be here tomorrow?"

"Yeah, I'll be here, Walter."

"See you tomorrow, brother." Then he turned and walked away. His mother would probably be pulling out of the driveway to get him just about the time he got home. He left the playground in the same manner each day when he simply realized it was time to go. He gathered his books, asked if I would be there tomorrow and walked away. On that particular day the last word really caught my attention. He used the word brother differently than I ever heard it before, simply meaning friend, but somehow it carried more weight. Walter always carried more weight. He played defense on the Chris Dillinger's of the world.

Chapter 2
Starting

Practically a man, I had already reached my thirteenth year when I made the starting line up of the eighth grade basketball team. I thought about my manhood while I pulled on a light brown pair of once white athletic socks. Almost certainly, Walter slept through detention while I mentally prepared for our fifteenth and final game of the season. Of course, it seemed a little strange not being in detention with him. We were both late getting back to class from lunch and only Walter received the honor of detention. I just got lucky this time. Something like that.

The team celebrated the schools best record in the last ten years: eleven wins, three loses, and an almost certain victory coming today against Morgan Junior High. We averaged fifty-five points a game through the regular season, and we were beating teams by an average of fifteen points. The ever improving jump shot of Walter Roberts contributed an average of twenty-seven of those fifty-five. Walter possessed a delicate grace on the court making him almost too mature for the game. Even last week, against Stony Hill, my fifteen points and seven assists were eclipsed by Walter's twenty-four points, ten rebounds. The tall thin frame that cast no visible shadows on the playground moved less awkwardly now, and cast one. The shadow was me.

"Yo, Smith. You have to read this." I did not even notice Walter come into the locker room until the book he threw me sailed halfway to my lap. "There's this crazy bunch of women who cut out their tongues in support of this little girl who gets raped, a transvestite football player, and a permanently disfigured college student. Although you couldn't quite tell he was disfigured until you saw my man in the little boys room." Walter laughed at the dilemmas of the characters in *The World According to Garp* by John Irving, as I read it off my lap. Interesting reading for a thirteen-year-old boy in detention. Always happiest when he just finished a book, Walter's energy filled the locker room, the way only his energy could. "You know Mrs. Rogers wouldn't ever be teaching that stuff in fifth period English. We'd take some serious notes on that." I used to ask Walter why he read so many books and he always claimed his mother forced him to read until he eventually started to like it. "I'd have to learn to like it or kill myself trying."

"You better get your mind off tongues and transvestites if you want to win this game today. There not just gonna roll over and die."

"They might as well do just that, Smith. For Christ's sake, it's Morgan. What'd they win? Like two games in ten years. Besides, Leo, it's just a basketball game. In ninety minutes we'll be showered and on the way out of our last season." No one could ever get Walter to take basketball seriously and it always bothered me. With so much talent and no desire to defeat opponents, his court values were incomprehensible. The way he loved to practice but could not care less about games changed the terms of competition. I believe only one person could spark his hidden competitive fire, and mirrors play terrible defense. How many thirteen-year-old kids do not care about winning and losing? I knew only one.

As usual, he was right, Morgan doubled as a canine training school. They came, they sat, they rolled over and they died. About an hour-and-a-half later, I walked out of the locker room where Sarah Parsons stood in the dark hall waiting for her son, Leo Smith. The grayness of the hallway resulted from an errant pass by a custodian who failed to notice a burnt bulb. The flat, white walls closed in on us, and the cool, caliginous hall felt like a dangerous place to end anything.

"Great game, Leo." I could never blame my mother for anything. In a short life filled with a few ominous endings in dark hallways, she stood at the beginning of every new corridor for better or worse, waiting quietly for me. The course of my life always determined by others, I often dreamed of the defining moment when this reality would change, and I could hold the reigns. I did not truly comprehend the complexity of what I asked, but I never would have asked to end the season in that hallway. With a gym bag on my shoulder, I walked away from the locker room and the season, down the hall, into the light.

"Your friend Walter is very good. You two play well together." My mother kept that wonderful grasp of the obvious as she began a conversation like any other mother would in her situation. You tell your child what they most likely already know in an effort to speak on the same level with them. To belittle a child is a natural instinct for most adults.

No predetermined intention of maintaining my silence entered my thoughts but my mind focused on other things. Endings are a strange and incomprehensible form of death, especially in the innocence of youth. The experiences and activities of my years were so limited an end to just one of them took away an entire part of my life. The emptiness of loss magnified the silence and I began to realize what it meant to care about something then lose it forever. I felt death and I responded to it. "Thanks for coming to the game."

Sarah Parsons drove the same 1988 black Jeep Wrangler for the last three years. The prototypical, midlife-crisis-mobile of the eighties could only be described by an eighth grader as cool. No matter what I ever thought of my mother, she made the same rebellious metamorphosis every time she shifted the gears and forced a strengthening wind to ripple the ragtop. I always believed the only eighth grader in the universe, whose mom owned a Jeep, slept comfortably in my bed. My thoughts shifted, with the gears, to new places and new things that were possible now that I once again experienced death. "Don't worry, Leo, you'll still be able to play next year in high school." Something about riding shotgun in the Jeep made my mother's uninformed statement an absolute truth.

We only shared a few words between the hallway and the driveway, where we piled out in front of the small, five-room, cigar box we called home. The lifeless, brown shingles reminded the world everyday of the very simplest things in life, while the decaying, white paint on the trim of each window asked politely for another coat to protect itself from the elements. The windows often reflected anguish and the screens knew much better days. The half-grass, which is half-grass, half-weeds, rebelled against each mowing with a stronger comeback than any blade could have anticipated. Our home offered the closest thing to architecture imitating life the town of Ledyard ever endured. I spent more time thinking about the word "home" than considering the idea of actually having one, and I am still not certain I ever figured it out. Can I believe that "home is where you hang your hat" or "home is where the heart is." Of course, clichés are the absence of original thought, so I hate them. For me, "home" exists as a mysterious place where the possibility of eternal happiness roams omnipresent and the only thoughts at home are those of love. In short, "home" constituted a fictional setting.

Our home, the small two-bedroom roof over our heads, could be best described as preparation for college dorm life. Time alone, privacy, a manicured lawn, neighbors named Fran and John, friendly dogs, and barbecues were all fables. The reality began with a caring woman who did everything she ever could to raise a son, and ended with a thoughtless son who never found the time to appreciate the woman.

I walked into my room and stared quickly at the posterized tongue of a dunking Michael Jordan. After a quick pump fake toward the blue shag carpet, I scored six uncontested points by dunking my sweat soaked tee shirt, basketball shorts, and underwear through the rim of my clothes hamper. I sat naked on the edge of my bed and held open *The World According to Garp*. The book lay under my eyes and above a not-yet-properly-used organ as I began to read. The room collapsed around me until there was only myself, inviting typed words and four walls. The greatest enjoyment in reading became clear upon the inevitable discovery of a character less fortunate than I. The disfigured college student Walter described would probably never sit naked and read a book again. Would he change his clothes without looking? Maybe he could shower with a jock strap on. Reading offers a young man a lot of important things to consider.

Chapter 3
Growth

I guess I just never understood served as the best answer I could muster as to why I never appreciated what my mother accomplished each day. Almost everything is beyond the grasp of a thirteen-year-old who thinks he knows everything, but at the more experienced age of seventeen, I finally understood that I knew nothing, now that was something. I appreciated a small pseudo-house in Ledyard, Connecticut, I appreciated brief moments of thought, I appreciated food on the table, and I appreciated Sarah. We passed on our chance to be the poster family for American values, but like all things, we evolved, we learned to understand, we learned to talk, and we learned to be the family we needed.

I also learned some of Walter's moves to the hoop, practicing on the blacktop, and waiting for my chance, while he started three of his four years at Ledyard High School. Finally, in our last season, I joined him in the backcourt. Walter still cared very little about winning and losing, but out of respect for the team, he made it seem as if he did. In the waning moments of a close game, the ball would usurp magnetic properties and find its way to the steel nerve of Walter Roberts, the outcome inevitable. Walter's life revolved around his mother, our friendship, books, and basketball, in that order. I knew that because he told me more than once. Scouts from various colleges would appear at every game our senior year and his apathy irked them. North Carolina, Duke, Georgetown, Michigan, and of course, The University of Connecticut all expressed interest in Walter's basketball ability. He feigned interest in their "big-time" courting and considered only UConn, and secretly Connecticut College, because he wished to stay close to home.

We still spent countless hours at the junior high school playground, and nostalgia remained constant in our lives. Sometimes Walter would scorch the pavement with my ass in a game of one on one, but mostly we shot jumpers and often Walter just read. Occasionally, I ceased shooting and just stared at Walter, while he concentrated on nothing but the page of written words. While lost in his thoughts, he appeared to forget the rest of us were with him. The red bandanna Walter always wore snugly on his head moved slightly as his eyes met the words, and thoughts were absorbed. He seemed oblivious to everything around him until he looked up and started a sentence with, "Do you think God knows..." or "If existentialism means..." The only thing that really changed over the years was the clockwork stops of Walter's mother. The black Honda never sped into playground parking lot in those later years. I think she knew her work was done.

"Week, did you ever notice that we don't have any friends?" The quiet, cloudy day should not have produced anything new, but a broken moment inspired a thought we never talked about. Walter and I spent more than three years in high school as misfits among the countless bodies searching for their clique, niche, club, or group. The social tenets of the American high school allowed starting basketball players the luxury of eccentricity, but Walter and I pushed the limits. In almost four years, I couldn't think of one person, other than Walter, I could call my friend.

"Of course, we have friends. If we don't have any friends you'll need to explain to me who all those screaming people are every time you score. This might be a ridiculous statement, Leo, but I'm willing to bet all those people know who you are. And if they're not concerned with who you are, I'm not sure those are the kind of people you want to be surrounding yourself with young man." This time, I couldn't quite buy into his rationalization or his sarcasm.

"You don't think it's strange."

"It's not so much strange as it is concentrated." He paused and stared, noticing the revealing look in my eyes conveying no understanding of his intentions. "How good are you at baseball?" He didn't wait for me to answer knowing I sucked; three years of gym class together proved that. "You don't really care though, do you?" He had the answer for that one too. "But, if you sucked at hoops, then you might want to get better at baseball. I don't need other friends because I've got you. If that drops me into the peasant caste of Ledyard high school, then I'll live with it. I'm a peasant. One of the things I'm most proud of Leo is the fact that I'm extremely happy with who I am, and what I've got. Before you begin seeking that which you don't have, you should take a nice long look at all the things you do have. If you can't find satisfaction in what is, *then* you should begin an examination of what you need. Life is where you find it brother." That was Walter Roberts at his finest on a day I'll never forget.

Sarah and I continued on our murderously-boring path as a mother and son who realized that "dysfunctional family" is redundant. She enjoyed her success at the hospital so her gray skies often broke for glimpses of a sunrise or a social setting. A few bold men dared to penetrate the atmosphere of the strongest woman I knew, and like excuses, there was something wrong with all of them. Generally, a recovering woman emerging from a midlife crisis and a confused teen with little direction are short on vocabulary for good conversation, so Sarah and I rarely spent time together. Most of our chats ended with bent ideas of a better life, the ends of rainbows, silver linings, a light at the end of a tunnel, and all that other crap. Our enabling fiction seldom led to new conclusions. We knew we were living much better than we had planned and around almost every corner someone lived worse. It's difficult to revel in the misfortune of others, so we respected it instead.

One slow, Saturday morning, when even cartoon characters appeared hung-over, Sarah and I engaged in one of our brief conversations. "Do you ever miss him?" Her startled look revealed she knew exactly whom I spoke of across syrup-soggy Eggos. More than three years had passed since either of us had seen my father, but my mother and I spoke with him on rare occasions.

"Leo, It seems like a place that never really existed. Every day I lose another memory, some small part of your father. Endings are always sad, Leo, and reliving endings can be even worse, but there is one thing I regret more than anything else."

She paused for a moment enabling the wall to fall down. "What's that? What's the worst thing?"

"I'm really happy he's gone. Isn't that terrible?"

"Yes." I smirked so she would not miss the joke. "I always hate it when you're happy." Sarah's guilty smile relieved her burden of regret and in the tick of the clock she removed him. I could not really share those emotions with my mother because I never knew how I really felt, no reaction at all. There's a void in a child's life when any constant becomes a variable. If you change his diaper, move his bus stop, paint his room, forget to fix his bike, miss his game, don't let him use the car, or deprive him of the male role model that every other kid seems to have, you just can't anticipate a standard reaction. These are life's little wonders. However, I never leave the toilet seat up, and I'll forever be able to lose an argument every twenty-eight days. That minute represented one of the longest conversations Sarah and I ever had about Richard Smith.

Chapter 4
Lecture

Walter and I marched through our senior year of classes and basketball with little difficulty. Unlike endeavors on the court, Walter and I were equally matched in the classroom. We both earned a few scattered Bs among a pattern of As. The basketball grades were straight As. We constantly argued with teachers, but rarely with officials, and scouts kept coming to drool over the "silky smooth swingman, Walter Roberts," as *Street and Smith's* worded it, and we just kept laughing. Walter might respond periodically to Princeton and Dartmouth, but UCLA and Kentucky never heard a word. I'm certain they never understood the same things their blue chip recruit did. Walter knew a 6'3" shooting guard would have to be exceptional to make it to the NBA, even more exceptional than him. He could be best described as an innovator, who always separated himself from the group with his original thoughts. He pictured himself using basketball for college, not college for basketball. Imagine that.

Months after our season ended, he walked toward third period English when I noticed him in the hallway strutting smoothly, and fashionably clad in Adidas sportswear from head to toe. I would have sworn, if asked, that he emerged from the womb with his black and white basketball sneakers on. Like his sneakers, the rest of his wardrobe consisted of mostly black or white clothes. I always took the time to critique his racially harmonious style telling him, "Us whites would never buy into his ploy." The one constant flare of color in Walter's garb was the red bandanna he loved to wear. His "hip homeboy" style meshed with his honor roll grades as a juxtaposition that made almost everyone around him self-conscious. Every once in a while I'd hear some peeved girl complain, "That Walter Roberts thinks he's all that." She uttered some sort of artificial expression for a person who really had their act together. Walter Roberts didn't think he was "all that," but he may have been.

"Week," I yelled down the hall to him before he could turn the corner into the next corridor. "Walter!"

"Hey, Smith. What's up?"

"Nothing's up, especially if we don't get to class on time. Then it's nothing but detention." Mrs. Carter suffocated students as the queen of the premature detention assignment. If denim was not actually touching the wood when the class bell rang, the unlucky student would find himself clapping erasers. No exaggeration, really clapping erasers. If you earned detention with Mrs. Carter you were an eraser clapping, broom pushing, silent reading, repetitive phrase on the blackboard writing, high school student at the pinnacle of misery. So we walked while we talked. "I wanted to catch you before class. Did you hear the announcement this morning about the prom?"

"The prom?" He's asked it like he would have asked "The coalmine?"

"Yeah, Week, you heard me correctly. The announcements have been echoing through homerooms for a couple days and my own mother's starting to give me heat about it."

"Smith, there's a few things you need to know." I recognized this particular brand of frustration having seen it before. "First, I hate the name Week. My mom hasn't busted my ass off the playground for about four years now so you can stop calling me that annoying name. Second, there's no way I'm shelling out three bills to take any girl from this school anywhere." I tried to stop him short but Walter was a locomotive when it came to his speeches. "Third, if your mom is giving you this much heat over the prom, why don't you just break down and take her."

Neither Walter nor I went on a date in four years of high school. I knew girls at school who were interested in me, and there were definitely young ladies ready to knock down Walter's door, but playing basketball under the lights or catching a late movie on the weekends always seemed more attractive. I liked girls, they liked me, but what the hell was the point. High school sweethearts are one in a hundred and three-quarters of those proclaimed "happily ever after" probably get divorced. Two things I loved as a young man: free time and money. Why waste both of them in one shot? Walter used to joke about curling up with a good book on a Friday night, and then for some strange reason, he did.

"Well, Week, you're not gonna believe this."

"I believe we'll be in detention this afternoon. I also believe you're walking a thin line addressing your loving brother as 'Week.'"

"All right, Walter. Enough with the name. You're never going to believe what I'm about to tell you. My mom is giving me heat for one reason but the rumor mill is offering another."

Walter bore a physiognomy that begged me, "get on with it, Smith" but managed, "Shock me."

"Well, two guys who spend all their time together and seem to have no interest in the swarming opposite sex around them can't simply slide through high school unnoticed."

Clearly, he did not yet understand my point. "We're suspect, Walter. People are talking."

"Screw you, Smith."

He turned away from me and quickened his stride as we approached the classroom door. "Listen, Walter, I'm going to the prom and so are you. It's still three weeks away and I know tons of unattached ladies who would love to go with you. We'll double date, clear the air and high school can once again be the stomping ground it was meant to be."

"Smith, who was I talking to when I said screw you?" Walter unveiled a punishing look in his eyes making his face almost unrecognizable. The look warned of something that resembled hate, not of me, but of the subject we discussed. People would miss the point if they thought Walter was homophobic, I don't think Walter Roberts feared anyone. "Was I talking to myself or was I talking to you? Listen to me. Never in my life have I been converted, confused, oppressed, ostracized, or in any other way affected by what any person said about the black, suspect, cursing, poetry reading, overachieving, gangsta-looking Walter Roberts you see before your eyes today. I don't live to make them happy, so they'll just have to find happiness on their own. You can't please the masses, Leo, and you can't save them. It doesn't work that way anymore. They have to be saved one at a time."

"Who said that?"

"I did. It's another Walter Robert's original. Get it? I'm going to class."

And suddenly, I did. Walter refused to accept one more stereotype in the very long line, while I saw an engraved invitation to the prom because I felt as if I needed to clear my name. Walter could have told me, right there in the hallway, all the secret reasons why I did not have to justify myself, but instead he let me discover on my own. It would be months later, when I unearthed the obvious answer, that my attendance at the prom made no sense at all.

"Hey, Walter!" I whispered from behind him as we entered the classroom. "Do you know that Susan Watts broke up with her boyfriend? She'd go in a heartbeat if I asked her. Remember that Weaver game?" Susan Watts, a cheerleader for the Colonels of Ledyard High School, invented new decibel levels screaming her head off when Ledyard beat Hillhouse for the basketball state championship. Walter used to joke that Susan cheered loudest and proudest for me, and his love for fiction and creativity did not make the story any less interesting in my humble opinion. He would reference the Hillhouse game by reminding someone that I scored seventeen points and dished out eight assists while leading us to the state championship as a senior. Of course, I'd mention that he poured in thirty points, grabbed twelve rebounds and scattered five assists, but he never would. He stopped to listen to the rest of my ranting, as he always did, and never explained the reasons why I did not understand.

Chapter 5
Nerves

During the course of the first date of my life, Walter Roberts sat home reading from *The Autobiography of Malcolm X,* his third time through Alex Haley's work. Walter claimed that Malcolm X felt a little embarrassed by the book explaining that his early life in Harlem was both glamorized and exaggerated. How would I know? Then again, how would Walter? I guess we all have our own opinions, in fact, a bright man might contend that there are nothing but opinions left.

I walked calmly along the sidewalk thinking how nice it would be to experience the power of any father awaiting his daughter's prom date. People talk money, business, politics, but does anyone ever feel that same power that her father feels on prom night. I waited silently on the doorstep of Susan Watts home looking up at the catbird's seat one step above. I picked up my tux at two, stepped into a barbers chair at three and devoted two painstaking hours to making my mother's eight-year-old, fading Jeep look presentable. The reflection in the glass of the outside door refused to tell any lies as I examined a young man who stood completely composed; completely composed of nerves. At six feet tall, going about one-eighty, I looked dashing in my penguin tails. At least that's what I kept telling myself.

Mr. Watts opened the front door and graciously invited me in the same way all prom fathers snare their quarry. Susan briefly explained in the preceding days that her father loved basketball and I now prayed for this small detail to grant me an advantage. Mr. Watts also frowned upon the idea that kids should get a free ride through school because they could put a ball through a hoop. He intended to gut me, grill me, and leave the pieces for the gulls. You can almost always see that look in a man's eyes. I'm sure, like most men in his position, he entertained no idea why he hated me, but as a daughter comes of age, it is the rule. Mr. Watts had no intention of letting some cocky kid leave the den unintimidated, precious daughter on his arm.

"Sit down, Leo." I complied. "The last time I saw you, you and your buddy, Roberts, were picking apart that Hillhouse High School defense. It's nice that basketball could end that way for you boys."

"Hopefully basketball is just beginning."

"That's one of the problems with athletics today. Kids start to focus so much on continuing their athletic careers they forget about academics. Take your buddy, Roberts, for instance. What's he going to do?" Mr. Watts walked out onto thin ice, and I felt a big crack approaching beneath me. He probably observed the Hillhouse game and made the association between Walter and myself. His assessment of Walter was naturally inaccurate, feeling the urge to clump people together into groups, and although the days of Uncle Tom and Nigger Jim were long since past reality, there were still strong beliefs in backwards, rural homes that black kids went to college on athletic scholarships only. "Probably head off to some Big Ten School, try to dribble his way through the classroom and have dreams of an NBA career."

"Mr. Watts, I had no idea you knew Walter so well. I was actually under the impression that he dropped out of high school when the basketball season ended and immediately began selling drugs to elementary school children. I forgot black folk had that second option of being athletes who waste their college education." I snapped. Mr. Watts, no one to me, somehow became everyone.

"Hold on, son, I'm no racist. I don't make the rules I just understand them. Things are the way they are." This unimportant, antiquated man knew he got to me. Probably a decent guy who just lived in a sheltered world, he would never throw a hood over his head and start burning crosses, but that didn't make him right. He didn't know Walter.

The conversation ended. I would have liked to finish it, but a stunning Susan Watts, momentarily unnoticed, stood in the doorway of the room. Always an attractive girl, her beauty on this occasion hit me like a back screen that never got called out. Replacing the air, she filled my lungs, as I not only lost my energy to argue with Mr. Watts, but my ability to breathe. She did not enter the room. Instead, she simply stood in the door and continued to pervade something cool across the air. She held a flawless pose for an instant inviting me to smile slightly and in that instant I forgot. I forgot everything. I did not gawk or drool, or move to accept her, I simply held her in my eyes and took my own detailed photograph of mind that I could always look back on and appreciate. Then I accepted her silent invitation, smiled, and moved towards her.

Mrs. Watts stopped us at the door, which now seemed smaller than when I entered, to capture a few photos of her own. Finally through the door, I took a deep breath of the cool night air that tasted distinctly cleaner than the smog in Mr. Watts house. We took only two steps into the yard before her father flipped his last two cents into our fountain of the coming night. "Be careful with my daughter. I know how prom night can get out of control."

I turned one-hundred-and-eighty degrees. "Be careful with ideas. I know how they can do the same." Susan's mother stood beside him, as a perplexed look contorted her face. "Good night, Mrs. Watts. We'll be careful." I spun back, turning away from the house again and brought Susan to the passenger side door of the Jeep.

Obviously confused, Susan asked, "What did you mean?"

"About what?"

"What you were saying to my father about how ideas get out of control?"

Always be vague first. "We'll your father had some ideas that he expressed to me that I didn't think were entirely true. I just didn't want his imagination or his mind to get out of control on the issue."

"What issue?" Susan made this particularly hard.

Lie next. "I just didn't want him to worry about you tonight."

"That was a sweet gesture, Leo, but it's not your fault. My father doesn't exactly see me as the picture of morality." As I unlocked the door, Susan kissed me on the cheek and it struck me as odd. Not the kiss, of course, because it could only be called sweet. I struggled with the fact that, at seventeen years old, a young cheerleader named Susan Watts made my history book as the first girl who ever kissed me. A slow, depressing grumble rose up in my stomach. In the night breeze, my body experienced that overwhelming feeling people only understand once they realize they've wasted precious time. Everyone does it; you just hate to think about it. I guess that same feeling will always remind me of the senior prom as my first real date.

As we drove out into the darkness, I made the decision that I would not tempt fate to suddenly jump into my life by thinking of all the things I should be doing. There were ins and outs to most social functions, but I cared very little. Susan Watts slowly became a nice girl in my eyes as we began our drive, and I noticed never really thinking about people in those terms. Nice, mean, sweet, funny, or whatever, people were just other people walking around me. I never thought about them, I'm pretty sure they never thought about me, but suddenly I drove along in a position to care. What I cared about most was not sacrificing Leo Smith to satisfy the needs of tradition or etiquette when it came to a prom date. I wanted to be myself so myself said, "You look absolutely beautiful tonight. I guess maybe I've never really thought to look at you in one way or another, but since I'm suddenly driving to the prom with you, and people are supposed to have all these ideas about one another, I guess my idea of you at the moment is that you're beautiful." I hoped that my honesty camouflaged my awkwardness.

"You really are different, aren't you, Leo?"

"I've never thought of myself in those terms."

I passed Susan Watts in the halls for four years and I never took time to find that amazing look on her face. She looked at me genuinely. In school, she always appeared to me as a sort of plastic mannequin designed to adorn the halls of Ledyard High. Suddenly she was real. "Maybe you should start thinking of yourself in those terms." And then came the bomb. "I'm kind of surprised you're here tonight, Leo. You know a lot of the girls around school were beginning to give up hope on Walter and you." I smiled at the idea of girls hoping, and ignored the insinuation. "Is he going tonight?"

"No, he's probably curled up with a good book." I couldn't help laughing at the truth. "Knowing Walter he's done with Malcolm X and halfway through Frederick Douglas."

"Who's Frederick Douglas?"

I showed no surprise. "I guess you don't hear about him too much in our history classes. He's a guy who made it." I drifted out of our conversation for six or seven passed mailboxes and thought about how Walter made me read that book. Then I began thinking about Covey, the slave breaker. I remember Douglass fought for his life with Covey, and the fight was worth it. Would Douglass have wasted a single fraction of his life contemplating the opinion of a man like Mr. Watts? Almost certainly not. Why did I? In many ways, I wanted to feel angry toward schools and parents and even Susan for not knowing who these men were. They fought for their lives, changed history, tore down barriers, and even found a way to casually slide into a great friendship. There stands a monument in Washington commemorating Lincoln, where is the one for the slaves he supposedly freed? All God's children? Of course, how far does my hypocrisy go? I never roamed the halls lost in thought, or scoured the bookshelves of the library searching for the faults of our forefathers and the great travesties in the history of our United States. Walter Roberts handed me that history and asked me for my opinion. I thought about the day Walter said, "White people are so ignorant." My friend sat at home alone on prom night knowing there are a lot of ignorant people; color has nothing to do with it. Ignorance, genius, discrimination, brotherhood, and almost everything else are based solely on ideas. Tomorrow Walter and I planned to go to New York City so we could discuss and decide on some of our own.

"Who was the last girl you went out with?" Her intrepid voice blended with the hum of the wheels churning over the pavement. I almost forgot Susan sat beside me. I knew her curiosity would spawn questions sooner or later so I stuck with the plan. First, be vague. "To tell you the truth, I don't really remember." The smell of the restaurant peaked past the radar of the most acute senses and already I faced trouble.

"I thought this was your first date." I should have congratulated her on finding the nicest possible way to tell me that me she knew. No less embarrassed by the large inadequacy other teens would have called a love life I appreciated the surreptitious nature of her gesture by flushing a deep red. "Oh, I'm sorry, Leo, I didn't...we'll actually I guess I must have wanted to embarrass you or I wouldn't have brought it up. I just wanted you to know that I thought it was kind of cool. I mean, I'm excited that you would choose me. Also, I guess I've gotten used to guys who expect things on the first date, and I can't see that being a problem with you." Frustrated with her twisted tongue she paused and held her head in her hands. "I'm sorry Leo." In the instant of her awkward recovery, I found a small chunk of salvation. Susan separated and concentrated, as her thoughts slipped away from the broad comparison between me, and all the other guys who came before me. Within a hair of an insult, she willingly exposed her singular focus on the young inexperienced man beside her. In the shallow depths of bucket seats, Susan did not wonder where her friends would dine, or if her ex-man moved comfortably in a back seat. She was here completely. In a luminous flash, transcending beauty, I began to notice her more deeply, as I would years later during stretched, soulful moments, as my first date.

We skidded through dinner held together by a prom bond, clinging to the small talk persisting as our only line of communication. We never resorted to discussing the weather, but in several instances that shift may have served as an improvement. In lulls of despair, I nearly allowed myself to believe that Susan wondered about the laughs her friends exchanged in the early evening, and how she ended up so far away. I dismissed the painful idea that she thought incessantly about where the old bastard boyfriend parked. Could she possibly continue to ignore all the little memories she might miss in the absence of her closest friends? Confidence brewed inside me that Walter made the greatest decision of his life. Could *The Autobiography of Malcolm X* offer any more confusion than this date? One for the city.

Dinner for two does not present the simplest solution for breaking the ice. I knew it, Susan knew it, and anyone within whispering distance of the table knew it. They probably knew it well. The walls of the restaurant closed in on us and the crisp mannerisms of *The Fish House* staff heightened the tension. I would have killed for McDonald's drive-thru and a decent CD. Dinner could not reach the table fast enough.

The meal saved our sanity by presenting a legitimate reason to break our mediocre conversation. Salad gave way to entree and the dessert cart passed us by. A very wonderful, quiet meal disappeared with my sanity as I prayed that Susan would not vanish permanently on her jaunt to the ladies room. Cash dangled in my fingertips insuring a shortened wait before the bill was settled. Walking from the table, I fostered no thought that Susan and I would ever feel uncomfortable together again.

We escaped the agony of dinner and I once again performed my gentlemanly duty opening the passenger side door. Susan responded again with a kiss, but this time she meant it. In that gentle message, she assured me the uncertain evening would go on. With a simple kiss, I suddenly believed she wanted to be there, and I believed in the soft grip of her lips she wanted me to want the same. What I wanted, and just now realized in a way I never before comprehended, was the young woman before me. I wished we would never break from this kiss holding me like a significant glance between passing strangers. A lot of questions needed answering, but in the space of her arms, the questions would have to wait, if only for a second.

"What was that for?" I could feel my face flush again as the first and most relevant question broke our new, excellent silence.

"It was to find out."

"Find out what?"

"Who cares what? I know what I needed to know." Susan basked in a position she forgot all about in her coarse exchanges with young men, she usurped complete control. I knew she wanted that and the fact of the matter stood naked before me, I wanted it too. Her whole teen life revolved around the wrong guy at the wrong time. Her vision actually penetrated the post-pubescent masks that young men wear, but she lacked the courage and conviction needed to ever change the pattern. The popular girls date the popular boys and to hide from that universal certainty meant risking the inflated status you spent twelve grades attaining. Susan did not hide from the truth in the restaurant parking lot. Instead, she walked right up and kicked it in the ass.

"Wow." My very small and self-conscious response clearly defined my thoughts.

"Wow is definitely a good start." Docile smiles from young girls are simply the best in life.

The most recent change of venue failed to hinder conversation as our comfort increased in the company of one another and Susan began what would unknowingly become one of the most pivotal conversations of my young life. "Leo, I have a question for you and I hope you're not offended because you shouldn't be." I immediately felt her uncertainty as she squeezed out a disclaimer that failed to help ease my newfound tension.

"I think you'd have to work pretty hard to offend me so go ahead and try your best." I did everything in my power to speak honestly over the course of our first date and I wanted her to do the same. I dredged through my mind attempting to ascertain what bit of dirt or personal quirk she would be exposing, but I drove the Jeep entirely unprepared for what followed.

"Well, it's sort of a personal question." She definitely found safe ground. I had no personal life, therefore the possibly of her asking anything even slightly embarrassing felt comical. She already knew of my inexperience with women, and my family life, dysfunctional as it may have been, floated far from embarrassing or offensive. I simply was not a mysterious person. Apparently, my peers thought otherwise.

"How close are you and Walter?"

"Best friends. Seems like we have been forever. What do you want to know?" She actually found one of my favorite topics of conversation.

"That's it. I guess that's all I wanted to know." The look on her face exuded something unmanageable in her mind, but explained nothing.

"That's the question. You were worried about breaching the tight secrecy of my friendship with Walter. That's not exactly what I would call a personal question. Everyone knows were best friends. All you'd have to do is see us in school and..." Suddenly, the look on her face changed from that of an inquiring date to one of a shameful schoolgirl. She failed to keep eye contact with me and I now grasped the impending direction of our dialogue. Happiness would not aptly convey the nature of my emotion.

"Oh Jesus, not you too. Why the hell would you go out with me if you thought I was a fag? Anger rose from my stomach reddening my pale face and the sudden explosion of violent words hindered my breathing. "You know just because we spend a lot of time together and we don't worship the cool castes of goddamned Ledyard High School, it doesn't mean we're gay. You know I should have expec—"

"Leo, please", her voice quivered. "It's not a big deal. I just heard some rumors at school-"

"Not a big deal! There are rumors going around school that I'm some kind of freak and it's not a big deal! So what was the date all about? Did you bet one of your friends that you could bring me back from the dark side? If it was a rumor about you, then maybe it would be a big deal! I can hear them now 'Oh my gosh, one of the amazing, cool clique might be gay. Somebody call CSPAN.' Don't fret though. It's only one of the weirdoes. It's no big deal."

"Leo, has anyone ever treated you differently?" She interrupted the way a parent stops the tirade of a small child. Her voice stopped me like a yank on my arm, warning, *enough is enough.* "No, they haven't! I've watched, Leo. I know everyone likes you. You won't even let someone get close enough to treat you fairly or unfairly, so why would it matter anyway? I thought other people didn't cut the mustard with you. And now you're so worried about what other people think, you're treating homosexuality like it's some sort of disease." She ceased avoiding eye contact and now glared at me relentlessly as if I shot from the grassy knoll. "It was just a question Leo. And no, by the way, no one ever dared me to go out with you. *You* asked *me* to the prom if I remember correctly. Don't you understand that in any high school two, very-good-looking, star athletes that never seem to have a date are going to fall under scrutiny. Nobody makes that rule, Leo." For that one split second she sounded like her father preaching "the rules of society."

"So I'm tried and convicted. You believe the rumors."

"It's not a fucking crime, Leo!" She raised her voice to a level I would have thought her incapable of producing, and somehow the vulgarity seemed appropriate. She gathered her emotions as quickly as she had lost them and continued. It was a question. I just wanted to know where we could possibly go from here. I like you, Leo. I like you for reasons that go beyond rumors and cliques, and fake ideas about who people are. I only asked because I thought it was a pretty good kiss. That's all.

Her questions shocked me less than her final statement. "A pretty good kiss." Had she actually said that? I breathed in my first compliment regarding sexuality, while Susan Watts loaned me a moment of silence.

Prejudice: the only next logical thought. From the first day, I counted Walter Roberts my friend I thought about prejudice, and the word always existed in the singular context of black and white. I guess just thinking in those terms represents pretty clear-cut discrimination. I felt naive for having once believed. I would never feel prejudiced again because of the color of my best friend's skin. Moronic! I did not know one homosexual person, not one single acquaintance, yet I immediately disassociated myself with "a group" because I feared what someone might think. I grouped people, and suddenly thought back to Mr. Watts in the comfort of his own living room. I guess a person can only hope to keep an open mind, give no guarantees, and prepare to fail all over again.

Susan and I calmed our raucous tones and continued to talk and forgive as I drove us toward the dance, and the rest of our evening. She understood that in a difficult moment I reacted with my fears rather than my ideals, and for that I remained sorry. Afraid Susan Watts had the wrong idea about me, I was quicker to defend myself than to realize she didn't judge me by my sexual preference. I knew about the rumors and they never truly bothered me until finally confronted: a microcosm for the very nature of the beast.

Presenting our tickets and walking through the doors, I saw the gymnasium as a passive martyr that died a death to save the dreams of young women who waited years for this day to come. "Together at Last" was our prom theme decimating hallowed ground where some of the most fecund events in my boring life took place. Silver streamers adorned the walls, balloons hid memories of cheering fans, and Louis Armstrong awaited his dance. "What a Wonderful World" replaced our National Anthem, a great theme song, but you just can't dance to it. I would remember my night with Susan, but I would strain to forget the feel, smell, and look of the gym on that evening.

We danced well together, if not in our aesthetic grace, at least in our continuing comfort. She talked with her passing friends as the songs played and the chaperons strained their vision through the dark gymnasium. I exchanged quick, meaningless hellos with each new acquaintance that stopped to tell Susan how gorgeous she looked, how great her dress was, and how they had voted for her as the prom queen. Susan seemed extremely comfortable while distanced from her friends. Any remaining tension dwindled and I convinced myself that somehow everything mysteriously turned out perfect. Of course, what comparisons could I make?

Off in a distant corner of my mind, I remembered how disappointed I became when Susan failed to recognize the name Frederick Douglass. Could her lack of knowledge regarding African-American history be any worse than my reaction to homosexuality? Doubtful. I never uttered a single, overt opinion at all on the issue, and she never read about Frederick Douglass. That did not mean I discriminated and it did not make her a racist. It meant only that in my juvenile years when I believed I knew all the mysterious answers; I actually left out some of the most important questions. Engaged in my deep thoughts, I accidentally stepped on Susan's foot, the most cliché of all my clumsy moves.

The jump back to reality forced me to acknowledge my excitement, and I noticed the magnificence of the feminine arms controlling me. I could almost hear the loud smile crossing my face when I thought about Susan, myself, and imperfection.

Christian Andrews and Shelly D'Angelo were named king and queen of the prom. In the ongoing tradition of royalty, they were perfect. High school girls loved Christian. The two-time captain of the soccer team, involved in seemingly every club, and a straight-A student was headed off to Dartmouth next year. In this gym, the decorated gym, it seemed only natural that people worship him. The kid was going places.

Shelly D'Angelo could only be described with several repetitions of the word beautiful. She kept guys awake late at night wondering why their last date looked like *Lucy*, of the missing link Lucy's, next to Shelly. They knew the answer as well as anyone else, everyone looked like a cave dweller standing next to Shelly. Upon meeting seventeen-year-old, female perfection Charles Darwin would have exhausted only four words to anyone within shouting distance, "I told you so." By comparison, Shelly lucked out as the only girl at Ledyard High who would never be calmly clubbed and delicately dragged away by the hair.

There were, however, issues keeping young Shelly frustrated and awake many evenings. She probably kept the lights on late more than one school night, baffled by the fact that algebra and geometry basically seemed like the same thing. She may have yearned to know the gender of Earnest Hemingway, but probably feared asking. Certainly no Einstein, and probably on her best day she could not have spelled Einstein, she worked from her strengths. The greatest of which was the fact that the average high school male rarely thought about girls with their brain, therefore never noticing Shelly's lack thereof. Hormones rage for young men and they usually raged in the direction of Miss D'Angelo. Boys thinking of Shelly or Shelly thinking of boys had nothing to do with brainpower. There lived a much stronger force. She watched from high ground in the American high school, but her destiny surely involved counterproductive things. As my thoughts subsided, I could not possibly contain yet another smile in the direction of the enchanting young woman with whom I danced.

"What do you think of Shelly D'Angelo?" Susan asked, having caught me in my previous stare, as we danced on. Susan could tell I thought of Shelly, but could not possibly fathom what content those thoughts contained. A little brainwashed by the norms of adolescence, my date believed boy's worshipped the beautiful in Big Brothers Ledyard High; they did not belittle them.

"She seems nice enough. She was in my math class last year. I don't see her working for NASA anytime in the immediate future." Unless they are short on airspace I thought to myself. "I guess she's a bit stuck on herself but that tends to catch up with girls who don't pass math or mirrors."

"You'd sleep with her in a second." Her voice wavered momentarily, but she showed no sign of anger.

"Who said I wouldn't?" Cool enough, I thought.

"You wouldn't even know what to do with a girl like her."

"Who said I would?" Undeniable. "What do you think of Christian? Would you sleep with him?" The game seemed easier when I did the asking instead of the answering.

"I usually don't think of him, but yes, I'd probably have sex with Christian."

"Me too."

"Very funny, Leo."

"An hour ago you wouldn't have thought it was very funny. In fact it probably would have confused the hell out of you." We laughed again as we would throughout the night whether we picked on people or envied them. Occasionally, Susan would kiss me causing discrete thoughts about memories I missed. I looked deep, with the passing of each overplayed prom song increasing the time we shared, and noticed over and over that Susan Watts was a great girl. Yes, I would have to say I liked her very much.

The windows of the Jeep resembled the glass of a freezer-frosted mug when it breaks the plane of the door and enters into the new air. I too commenced breathing something new. When I moved awkwardly, Susan waited patiently, and things were slowly, neatly, sometimes arduously, becoming warmer. Consumed with expectation, I remained unsure where the motionless Jeep would take us. Susan, now a cartographer, experienced feelings she never grappled with before. Her date completely innocent, trying his best, it must be a first. Rather than pound on a jury box, or cross-examine witnesses to prove my innocence, I fumbled yet another attempt to unhook Susan's bra. Instead of smirking or laughing, Susan wrapped her right arm softly around my neck and completed the botched unhooking with her left. I felt the slight change in her chest through my "U2" T-shirt she had donned less than an hour ago. She seemed to glide around the back seat of the Jeep in my nylon basketball shorts while I lunged and panted seemingly caught in quicksand. I convinced myself of only two things; Susan grasped complete control, and more importantly, she loved it.

I gave her the shorts and T-shirt, as well as a soon discarded sweatshirt, out of the gym bag I always kept in the Jeep. She asked without reason or embarrassment if she could change out of her ridiculously uncomfortable dress on the ride to wherever. As any gentleman would, I kept my eyes on the road, and the rear view mirror, as she changed in the cramped back seat. An interesting little game we played, I pretended not to look, but did, and she pretended not to catch me, but did. I played the visiting team adjusting to her home court. Thank God, no crowd. Once changed, she motioned for me to drive down a dirt road approximately three miles from the school. I couldn't possibly object, but had to wonder.

"Why are you doing this?" I asked softly, trembling through a deliberate groan.

Susan kissed my neck in a way that made it feel like she kissed every part of my body, and the floor of the Jeep enjoyed sharing the energy she created through my toes. Suddenly she halted to answer my ridiculous question. "I sort of figured you might be enjoying it. Sorry your not."

"You know exactly how much I am enjoying this. Not just now but this whole night. What I mean is...Well, why are you with me right now?" Like a lot of questions that I asked within the constraints of a short lifetime, I really did not want to know the answer. I wanted reassurance but feared she could not provide.

"It's refreshing, Leo. It's nice to spend time with someone like you." Uncertain whether she complimented me, or insulted, I listened. "I just mean...Well...I've never had sex with a virgin before and it seems like..." I promised myself I would later admit I never heard a word she said after "sex." In that incredibly brief lapse of time before I jumped on top of her, I thought about the fact that she was fun, sharp, attractive, very attractive, my first date, my first kiss, and my first...Then came the part where I jumped on her.

After another five minutes or so of romping around the back seat, the skies seemed to light up red, and then for a moment blue and then back to red again. A weakness for grammar school mythology allowed me to think *Fireworks?*

Could it be that good? Then the sky definitely lit up red, white, and blue. I wasn't feeling very patriotic under the changing, colorful sky, neither was Susan. We instead felt caught, very caught, and the officer methodically moved toward the Jeep while I struggled to put my shirt on and Susan nonchalantly kicked her bra under the seat.

I rolled down the window and tried my best to convince. "What seems to be the problem, Officer?"

"I hope your kidding. License and registration please." I struggled to find the registration in the glove compartment and almost laughed thinking of the officer's tone asking for the documents. That one line is probably the only real thing on television. "Leo H. W. Smith. I won't be so incredibly bold as to guess what on earth you're doing out so late, Mr. Smith."

"We were just watching the stars, Officer." Susan snickered and we both glared at her knowing the humor of the situation should not be recognized. She could laugh because somehow it's never the obligation of the promiscuous young lady to speak to the police.

"Please step out of the car, Leo." I stepped out onto the dirt road and followed the officer away from the safety of the Jeep toward the roman candles and bottle rockets. "Now, Leo, I'm going to take a quick stab in the dark here if you don't mind. I'm no detective so you're going to have to stop me when I go wrong." I nodded cautiously before realizing I did not need to respond. "Ledyard prom? Big date? Inconvenienced by an officer of the law?"

His sarcastic expression now called for a response. "Yes, yes, and yes."

"I understand your problem, Leo, but you need to get out of here before someone comes along who cares very little. Go on home for the night. Somebody's parents will go away for a weekend in a week or two and you'll get your big chance. You always do." The officer smiled and turned back toward his car. I opened the door of the Jeep before the officer issued his last warning. "Be careful, Leo."

"Yes, sir, speed limit all the way."

"That's not quite what I meant. Good night." The officer climbed into his car and pulled away slowly. Getting back into the Jeep, I blinked my eyes and refocused on the clear picture of failure and bringing Susan home.

Susan's last chuckle turned into hysterical laughter. "You should have seen the look on your face."

"And, of course, you were calm, cool and collected. Dad would have loved to see you come home in a squad car. Then again, I guess you have nothing to worry about, he probably would have blamed me."

"That's not true. He actually would have shot you."

We made fun of each other for the rest of the ride. The feelings and actions were all very new to me, and in some small way I suppose we both experienced something new that night. As we rolled to a stop in front of her house, we both looked forward to spending more time together. One year shy of voting privileges, I looked at the unscathed virginity of the whole experience as something completely different.

"Do you want to do something tomorrow? It's supposed to be beautiful out. We could go to the beach or just walk in the woods or something. A picnic?" Not the offer, but the sound of a woman's voice making the offer, raised small, fearless goose bumps for the last time in the course of an incredible evening.

"Actually, I'd love to do all those things with you, but Walter and I are going to New York tomorrow. He wants to pick up some CD that hasn't been released around here yet. I never know what that kid is going to spring on me next." I barely heard what I said while I silently wished without words that Susan would never get out of the car.

"New York for a CD?"

"That's Week."

"What's weak?"

"A story for another day. Walter and I have been brothers for a long time." I knew without thinking that I uttered the second statement for myself, so I recovered. "Hey, I'm not going to come back tomorrow night and find you without your glass slipper am I?"

"You should be so lucky." For one reason or another I believed she cared about me and I couldn't resist the obvious temptation. I leaned across the faded interior of the Jeep, which had seen almost everything, and kissed Susan Watts one last time. She looked up at me after the embrace with content eyes that appeared on the edge of tears. I stroked an eyelash off of her cheek and enjoyed the tranquil quiet of the last moment of my first date. She closed the door of the Jeep and walked up a lighted brick path to the safety of her father's home. She looked back only once and that look meant everything. I closed my eyes to get a perfect picture of a strong girl named Susan Watts, now gone from my life.

Chapter 6
Pain

Random thoughts of Susan Watts continued to fill my head as Mrs. Roberts black Honda raced down I-95. Occasionally, I would disclose some incoherent nonsense to Walter about a night that could only be called my entire love life. I told him about our awkward dinner, our slow dances, our first and last kisses, and, of course, of the man in blue who spoiled the mood. I could clearly see Walter's expression of legitimate happiness, but he would not resist a few jabs at my newfound emotions.

"So, when's the big day Casanova? The ring will set you back more than the three bills you willingly dropped on the first date. I think a nice conservative girl like Miss Watts will accept no less than one carat and the vision of our hero on his knees." His laughter always served as one of the greatest joys in my life, even when it came at my expense.

"Screw you, Week." I relied on the one word that would forever unsettle the tranquil mood of Mr. Roberts.

"Snappy come back, Casper."

"Listen, Week. You know you're dragging, my staying out all night, never getting to bed, waking up at six o'clock in the morning ass all the way to N-Y-C. Can't you at least tell me the purpose of this lengthy mission?" Our volume surpassed the sound of the radio when we began taking thoughtful cheap shots at one another.

"Smith, you're forgetting. My town. My people. My atmosphere. Just enjoy the ride and we'll get there soon enough."

"Now you're really reaching. You know damn well that you haven't been to the Apple but three times in your whole sheltered life. How is this *your* town?"

"But you are forgetting once again, my silly, maladjusted, hung-over-with-love friend, I'm black." Walter's face beamed with his last comment because even at my sharpest I could not argue with that. However, the holes in his logic remained fair game.

"You are correct, my friend. I forgot all you Negro types know your way around each and every one of those 40-ounce ale-houses, vile-at-the-door, crack houses, and most importantly the gang hang outs. I sure do hope it is white boy day." Sarcasm thickened with the traffic. "Now that I think about it, Geeves, I believe I might recall a sign we passed a little while ago that said, 'Crack House Open House.' Yes, yes, I'm certain I did. Drive on, my good man, tallyho!"

"Smith, will you please turn up the radio so I can drive and you can think about your wife and scribe copious lists of cute baby names, you white-picket-fence-dreaming moron." As long as I had known him, Walter never believed in ending a slightly heated discussion without the last word.

"You're such a clever Negro."

"Radio, Leo! Radio!" We continued on our way, which is to say, on our path, and with our insults. Humor surfaced as my first thought when I reflected on how Walter and I always seemed to continue on our way, even chuckling aloud under the sound of the music. Much like this trip, I guess people never know exactly where they are going.

Some people get there and some people don't. On this day it seemed, for some reason, special to be doing it this way, with a friend I mean. Walter and I always moved onward together and I believed, as the car sluggishly shuffled along, that we always would. I imagine one of the greatest things about being best friends is that once in a while you think about it, and understand the real importance. There you are involved in a predicament, argument, labyrinth, or road trip, and you realize that the greatest times of your life are shared. Without warning you know how sad you would be if your friends missed this, whatever *this* is on a particular day. Maybe you're exchanging your vows, maybe you're laying a friend to rest, and maybe you're traveling southbound on Interstate-95 with no predictable destination.

Walter and I allowed the remainder of the ride to pass without much conversation. We just listened and thought as we battled occasional traffic headed for the city. For me, the city existed only as a strange and secret place where mysterious, frightening, and unthinkable events occurred. I had no idea what made it so secretive when millions of people meandered along the sidewalks everyday. Most of those people probably never sequestered a secret in their life, they all hid their own, the most treacherous, but nobody really guarded the ones revealed in confidence. People who have secrets all share that same look, it's the look someone has when they slip on the ice in a crowded parking lot. You think everyone is watching you but no one actually notices. People in New York mastered that look without even trying. At the moment so did Walter Roberts.

"What's up, Walter?"

"What do you mean?" Clearly defensive.

"I don't know, you just have this look on your face like something is wrong. I figured I'd ask."

"Hey, can you read that sign up there?" And it clicked.

"Unbelievable, Week. Those very tall buildings right over there look a lot like New York and you can't find your way onto the island. I'm not so sure the folks on this street, you know, *your people*, will extend their open arms and undying love to help you. We look like we're about ten blocks from where were supposed to be."

"How the hell would you know how many blocks we are from anywhere?" We were definitely lost. "Besides we're not even lost, you only think we're lost. I know for a fact that if we take this left up here we're right back on track. You forget my friend you are dealing with an A student." Walter constantly attained A's and took pride in his grades, but in this instance he made a more specific reference. Last Wednesday he beat me on our final history test by nine points. His grade belittled his peers as the only A in the class, and I heard about that letter for three games of H-O-R-S-E that afternoon. "I'd better lead the way."

"I would agree with you completely, my historically-knowledgeable friend, but unfortunately you defeated me on a history exam and I seek an expert in geography. If you would like to stop and ask for directions we could do that but you'll need a 100 on the next Spanish exam."

"You know, my dear, little, white-boy Leo, that almost sounded racist."

"Not racist, wise ass, lost and truthful."

"Well, when I *necesita tu ayuda* I'll ask for it. Until then, shut up or expound on the details of your lovely new girlfriend."

"I believe it's "necesito" and she was great." He knew I'd shut up about geography if he let me enlighten him on my sex-ed class. I provided him with the major plot lines already, but in the face of my own small history last night signified a revolution, or at least a movement, so I shared the details. By the time I connected the skirmish with the cop and the fiasco with the bra into one long run-on sentence, I think Walter really became interested in the story.

"I wondered why you weren't wearing that U2 T-shirt. I figured you'd wear it since it's the only black article of clothing you own and you'd want to look NY hip. In my ignorance, I'd forgotten who wears the cool Ts and *the pants* in the family. After all, Leo, what's yours is hers and what's hers is hers. You got that all figured out now, boy." Walter remembered the shirt because I purchased it when he and I actually went to the U2 concert together. I dragged him the whole way to the ZOO TV show, but I'll never forget the look on his face during "Pride." During the song, Martin Luther King is projected delivering his "I Have a Dream" speech on a screen five stories high. I always loved that song, but when it played that day in concert I wondered about a lot of things. How many fans in Foxboro Stadium knew that King was killed on April fourth in Memphis? The facts were right in the lyrics so any of the listeners could have figured it out. Then I wondered how many people knew about the black security men who were removed from their post across the street. What about the tree blocking the view from where the shot was supposedly fired? Roosevelt Tatum? Charles Stevens? The numbers were dropping. How many of them knew about a conversation between two friends on a playground many years before that concert? And then I was back in the car.

"Remember I had to drag you to that concert. You thought if it wasn't rap, classical, or jazz, then it just wasn't music. What Irish band could throw tunes? 'Damn bagpipes' were the exact words if memory serves. The poor, misinformed, socially closed out Walter Roberts of old. Don't worry about the black shirt, Walter. You've got enough black on for both of us." Walter did not believe in surprise when it came to his garb. Today the black, nylon, Nike sweat suit represented the everyday wear he might don for the court or the classroom. "Comfort and style," he would happily explain to anyone who asked.

"Smith, you'll just never understand my stylish ways."

"I understand that funky looking red doo rag on your head is crooked as hell." Vintage Walter.

"Like I said, Smith, style. Hey how were her friends at the prom? Were they all bent that Susan had the audacity to show up with the inexperienced, untouchable, out-of-the-clique likes of you."

"Actually, Week they created their own little opinion of me long before the court was announced. Both of us for that matter." I began to explain, as Walter looked down the road, not quite bewildered, but at least distraught. I explained the exact perceptions that Susan's friends constructed about the two of us. We seemed like really nice, good looking, likable, athletic guys with lots of promise, but perhaps no motivation. At first Walter thought I meant lazy, but I clarified the misunderstanding, explaining that in most social circles we were in fact, questionable. "It's just like I told you in the hallway, brother, people were talking. Jesus, look at this neighborhood. Man, I don't think were in Kansas anymore."

"I'll get directions." Walter parked the car along side a convenience store, stepping out into Oz without another word. Exiting the store less than thirty seconds later, the disgruntled look on his face offered the information before he could.

"No dice?"

"Actually, I bet you could find dice all over this hood, but Vasco De Gama set sail. I'm going to check with his mates around the corner." My feet hit the pavement and I fell into stride with Walter after closing the car door.

"I'm telling you, Walter, you should have gone to the prom with me. Who knows, you might still be *questionable*." I started laughing as we continued down the street. "Don't worry man it's just a rumor and after the prom I'm sure nobody even believes it anymore. Of course you might still have problems getting a date around Ledyard. Imagine that, two guys like you and me being gay." I continued laughing but Walter failed to see the humor. Neither of us wanted to be lost.

"Leo."

"Yeah. What's up, Walter?" He looked at me with a stoic expression conveying little of what he felt. His face changed slightly as his brow furrowed and he prepared to speak. The newest expression seemed defined by fear, but in a second I knew that was impossible, Walter feared nothing. He broke his stride in a military turn and squared his shoulders to face me completely.

"I am gay."

"Yeah, me too. Come on, seriously what's up?" His obvious agitation grew as we faced one another on the street. Walter loved controlling every situation and for him, losing his way meant losing control. "We'll figure out where we are. It's not like we're on a schedule. Hell, I don't even know where you're dragging me."

"Will you shut the hell up and listen for a second!" For the first time in our lives he raised his voice to me in tone of disgust and in one second, one heartbeat, one statement, I knew that my friend Walter Roberts meant what he said. And from there my brain ceased functioning.

"What?" I shouted without intending to. "What the hell are you talking about?"

"I've been thinking about it for a while now and I really thought something was wrong with me. Now I understand there isn't anything wrong, it's just who I am. I'm ready to accept that. Everything people have been saying is true, but you know that doesn't matter to me. I just needed to tell you. I know it doesn't really change anything and it was ridiculous to hide, but you're my best friend, Leo. I just figured you should know the truth."

Only a brief moment of agitation kept me from reacting instantly. My mouth began without ever processing the information and my words were filled with animosity. "Friends? I don't even know who you are. You've been lying to me for God knows how long and now you drag me to New York to tell me you like guys. How am I supposed to react? The only true friend I've ever known has been living a lie, and now he needs me. Who the hell do you think you are dumping this shit on me?"

"I'm your brother. That's who I am. This doesn't change anything. I don't want you to change. I don't want to change. I just needed to tell you and I would have told you sooner if I was even sure myself. Today seemed like the right time. The whole time you were beaming about your earth shattering night with Susan, I tried to figure out how to tell you. I wish I could understand your evening. I wish I could see Susan the way you do. Not for my sake, but for yours. I'd love to understand but I don't. That doesn't mean I don't hear you or that I can't listen. Nothing changes."

"So what do I do? Just give you a kiss and tell you I understand."

"No, but you can stop being an asshole and tell me you're my brother." Walter's eyes darkened with the midmorning sun at his back and something in those eyes made the alley, the street corner, and all the bricks of the building disappear. I pieced together something in his eyes that made me ashamed, and collapsing under that look, I turned away. With my back to Walter, head hanging, I could see his shadow spread across the pavement reaching my feet and beyond. "Are you my brother?" He asked with simplicity and calm. A passive expression dominated my face when my brain waves bounced again, and three words filled my mind. *Too many years*. I looked down at the ground and found myself engulfed in the shadow of my brother Walter Roberts and thought about one day of two-on-two at the playground and each astonishing day since. He never knew I smiled as he asked again, "Are you my brother Leo?" I thought to myself how Walter and I would always be brothers, the greatest certainty in my life.

When I turned to answer, a sharp noise shattered the silence of the street. The sunlight forced my eyes to close partially as I looked at Walter and my brain decoded the noise. The shot came from the corner of the building in the direction of Mrs. Robert's car. As his knees buckled helplessly and he fell to the ground, I began to see the blood streaming down his now expressionless face. The whole scene seemed impossible as my thoughts drifted from the playground to senior year in that instant of denial. The gunshot hit Walter in the side of the head, and the red bandanna hit the pavement softly only a second after his face. I escaped my frozen trance and moved to Walter's side as a blue speck bobbed away, running in the distance beyond the corner. I turned Walter onto his back and held him in my arms as his last breaths escaped his unconscious self. In the last beat of his pulse, I pulled Walter's head close to my chest and begged him not to go. The street widened and the sun would not fade on this day of darkness, while I knelt in the alley alone, watching my brother Walter Roberts die. Together, for the last time, with his head resting in my arms, blood soaking into my shirt, I realized that he never heard my answer to his last immortal question. Through streams of unyielding tears, I answered him that morning as I have every day since, "Yes, Walter, I am your brother."

Total dismay usurped complete control of my body sitting in the police station for the next and worst hour of my life. The station felt fictional and the men who filled it followed suit. Without much light or hope, the building seemed like the end of the world instead of part of it. I tried with all the fleeting energy in me to gain strength. In the next five minutes, I would call Mrs. Roberts and tell her that the majority of her world, like mine, died on a trip to New York City.

My second altercation with the police in the last twenty-four hours surpassed pain and I wished, without believing, that I would awake from this malignant dream. I needed to know why it happened. Why could this happen to someone who did nothing wrong, someone with everything to lose, someone like my friend. In that last hour I saw visions of Walter playing basketball at Princeton, or UConn, or in a playground three-quarters of a mile from my house. I thought of concerts, Dean's lists, and a future. He *was* talent. He *was* pride. He was gone. "Are you Leo Smith?" The voice seemed very faint as it drifted down from above. I slowly looked up at the uniform eclipsing the precinct walls and nodded my head.

"You never know who's gonna be next around here." He spoke in a matter of fact manner as if he were not talking about a person. "I'm Officer Starick. I have to ask you some questions about what happened this morning." The officer failed to tuck in part of his shirt when he dressed and that part of the sum exemplified him best. His best days behind him, he managed to grow into the stereotype proliferated in every corner doughnut shop. The man failed to exude any quality that made me feel safer having battled a mean city for many years and having lost that battle.

He explained that Walter was shot and killed by a gang member who mistook his bandanna for "colors." They put together no definite leads, only a possible gang they could question about the slaying. Walter Roberts, my friend, shot for no reason at all. Someone thought he crossed an imaginary line where he should not, and in an effort to defend "theirs," and play God, someone took his life. I heard only a few words the officer said.

After a brief interrogation, which left me believing the gunman would never be found, I made arrangements to catch a train that would bring me to New London, an officer would bring me to the station. On my way out of the personified misery, Starick stopped me to stab me with a few more words. "I'm really sorry about your friend, Leo. It's a shame that what's cool in Connecticut is deadly down here. I don't know why they're like that. It's a good thing they're not all gang members." Starick turned slowly and walked away. Disgusted, I walked toward the pay phone knowing that I needed to call Walter's mother. Rethinking Starick's words a thousand times in those fifteen steps, I remain certain that I never hated a man again with the ferocity I felt in that precinct.

"Hello, Mrs. Roberts?"

"Leo, are you okay? How was basketball?"

I sat in the bus station alone, with one thought tearing at me the same way it would for the rest of my life. I neither had, nor wanted a release from the thought of one unanswered question. I would never forget Walter and I would never forgive myself for leaving my best friend uncertain. Motionless and terrified, I contemplated his last breaths of mortality knowing he may have felt alone. Walking from the stage, I was a poor player who forgot to deliver his last line, ending the play miserably. The last line for my friend who sought confirmation in the whirlwind of disbelief that accompanies a rigid realization that your time has come. Failing to offer assurance, I lost my friend. I lost a safe and wonderful part of my life. In the single worst moment of my insignificant existence, I lost my voice.

Book II
LEO SMITH

Chapter 7
Fear

"I'm sympathetic with your problem but quite honestly I don't care what happens. Why don't you just fire him and get a new night watchman. That bastard brought all this on himself." Sarah balanced on the brink of explosion just minutes into a conversation she never believed she would have. With his newfound apathy clearly in control of his body and mind, Leo could barely hear his mother's voice through the walls. "My son and I have done fine without him, so maybe you can find a way to go on without him too. I just can't see any reason we should be involved." She had not heard from the Fortuns since Leo and she left The Grand Hotel shortly after the divorce.

"Sarah, believe me, we do understand, but we think if Leo could come see him, Richard would be able to get back on his feet." Margaret Fortun was a strong woman, persuasive when necessary and callous when challenged, but she now embraced an unstable subject at a bad time: a rough combination. "He's been with us a long time, Sarah. We can't just abandon him and neither should you, no matter what he's done. I think he misses his son." Margaret believed a compassionate, understanding Sarah would ignore old wounds, submit to the request of a one-time friend, and come to the aid of a former love. The answers to those questions were no, no, and no.

"He's my son, Margaret, and quite frankly you have no idea what Leo is going through right now. His best friend just died in his arms. I don't think he's ready to be saving souls just yet." Sarah felt the tears on her cheeks as plainly as she felt the futility of trying to hold them back. Emotions flowed freely from her battered heart as brand new pains surfaced from places which long since ceased to hurt.

"Sarah, we'd just like you to have Leo call. He's not a child anymore and perhaps he could make the decision himself." Miss Fortun suspected she would not bend a now iron-sided Sarah Parsons and wanted to talk to Leo himself. She sensed the cracks in the hull give way and hoped her message would get through.

"I'm certain Leo will feel the same way I do. I know my son and if..." Margaret did not allow her to finish.

"I'm sure you do know him dear, but the choice should be his. Understand this, Sarah, Richard can't keep up his behavior. Leo has to be aware of what his father needs, and then he can decide on his own if he wants to desert Richard." A cheap shot atypically asserted from the normally passive old woman, but nonetheless effective. Sarah would never forget but she could always forgive; a characteristic that pervaded her soul, and as genetics dictated, it passed on to her son.

"Margaret, you have to understand the timing. Richard Smith is the deserter, not his son. At this point he can drink himself straight to a warm vacation in hell. Leo is my concern now." Sarah became furious and felt ridiculous succumbing to the tears caused by a phone conversation that threatened no one. Only mothers know the feeling. A long time passed since she last considered the well being of her old flame and she took pride in the significance of memories disappearing.

Unfortunately, every ex-wife has a little room left in their heart. It just happens.

"Just tell Leo. Believe me, I wouldn't call if it weren't important. Things are different now Sarah."

"Goodbye, Margaret."

"Take care of yourself, Sarah."

"Always." Sarah hung up the phone and wiped away the last of the few tears marking her face with resentment. She never completely lost her love for Richard and the conversation revived some memories of him as a good husband. Margaret Fortun failed to understand that Sarah lost her trust for Richard, not her love. The kitchen walls of her Ledyard home reflected an unyielding revelation, and now the most difficult thing for Sarah was the truth. The truth that in both the shallow and deep recesses of a young heart, a son wonders about his absentee father; the truth that despite all his own pain, if he thought he could, Leo would help. The idea that her son might soon leave her hung in the tornado of a dangling phone cord now disconnected from a young man's future.

Sarah Parsons did not sleep well that night as nightmares wilted in the presence of this mother's newfound reality. Her seventeen-year-old son suffered with a lot on his mind, a lot more than he should. Sarah knew that in the following days confusion would come to dominate Leo's life as alchemistic options clouded his mourning heart. Leo spent unrealistic hours trying in vain to comfort Walter's mother, telling her how he died beautifully as if he could see before him a better place. He explained her son's eyes were full of peace and harmony. He explained that the brief, shallow breaths he heard in the last seconds expressed calm and acceptance. In short, he lied.

Despite his efforts to visualize the end, Leo could not remember what happened in that alley. In his most succinct thoughts, he only remembered a brush with the cold from that eighty-degree afternoon; he remembered the chill. Sarah knew Leo would try to comfort himself, as his independence existed second only to his co-dependence with his friend. Healing alone through day and night, he sought the help of no one else. A few teammates and acquaintances stopped by the house to offer condolences, simply because they thought it the thing to do, but they were stopped at the door. Even Susan Watts was turned away. Leo refused to see anyone. Sarah, unable to explain the pending lesser tragedy, thought it best to continue hiding the last straw. Soon she would have to tell Leo about his father, but that moment could be delayed until after the funeral. Somewhere, huddled deep beneath her concern for Leo, Sarah began to feel her own dreaded fear proliferated by thoughts of living without him. She accepted herself as strong, but could not contain her worry.

Finally, hiding in the chaos, she found a nanosecond of normalcy realizing a rented tuxedo cuddled closeted somewhere in the house. Amid tempestuous conditions, she found time to forgive herself for never asking her only child one simple question, "How was the prom?"

Three days passed easily in the outside world and painfully for those who still failed to see the Almighty's greater plan in the death of a talented young man. Leo punished himself continuously with thoughts of the brotherhood that ended without certainty. Stability seemed out of the question when coupled with Mrs. Roberts' request for Leo to serve as a pallbearer. Leo sat in his room staring at the most appropriate thing he could find. *The Free-Lance Pallbearers,* he read off the wrinkled, deep purple cover in front of him, one of the many books his friend handed down. Scared, he thought to himself, the word above all others to describe him on the day before sanity would be put in the earth.

Sarah continued to pry wisdom from her decision to keep Richard Smith out of Leo's elaborate equation. She justified her choice by continually citing her son's best interest on the footnotes in the back of her mind. Naturally, her own needs fit the equation as well, but she refused to do the math. "Tomorrow," she thought. Leo split his time evenly between the sequestered comfort of his room and the undeniable travesty engulfing the Roberts' house. He offered everything he could, denying Mrs. Roberts only when she asked that he deliver the eulogy. He accepted that he could only keep his composure from breath to breath with no guarantees, and funerals rarely need more sorrow. While people understand, no one is ever happy with the broken spirit who in the last moment of weakness flings himself onto the casket.

On the third day a young man with limitless dreams would be put in the ground. The final destination served as the ultimate contradiction in the eyes of so many people who witnessed him soar. Many of the basketball players came to the funeral with a few other scattered classmates. Ultimately, no one could deny that this young man died with anonymous admirers and few friends. Leo barely felt the hidden comfort that Walter chose to live this way. Convinced she did something wrong in her limited relationship with Leo, Susan Watts did not attend and no one missed her. She stayed home and offered a short, ambiguous, non-denominational prayer for Leo Smith. Leo lived, in a brief span, as the rock where everyone could cling, knowing that in the space of those silent hours there is little need for more people to mourn. He mouthed the words without a sound and never shed a tear, "I will mourn when I'm alone." He owed that.

Leo prayed in the church repeating a one-word query without physically disclosing his growing trepidation. He carried the coffin bearing the weight of his best friend then noticed each curve when the funeral procession passed through Ledyard. In the last seconds, feeling very much alone while others hung on the words of a priest who hardly knew the deceased, Leo prayed again. He did not pray for "the face" at the playground, though in many ways, the words could only be understood by his brother. He prayed for everyone else. He prayed against brotherhood. He prayed against love. He prayed against human understanding, against devotion, against loyalty, against selflessness. He prayed that no man on earth would ever feel for another the way he felt for his brother. Then, and only then, could they avoid this feeling of loss. When he grabbed hold of the brass, he revoked his prayers and thanked a God he believed in more fervently than ever, for each day he spent with his friend. If it had only been that first spring day of glorious victory on the playground, it would have been sufficient, but the evolution produced so much more. The wind cooled the day as the leaves blew to escape the malicious sun in the continuing cycle of nature. Yes, it was true. Even on this day the birds bellowed their loquacious daggers signaling the world that life would go on without him. Grass grew and the trees bent to catch the sunlight along with the knees of those who clung to their loved ones for support. Leo wanted to believe that everything, not just everyone, could feel this pain when for the first time in his life he helped his brother *down*. Then, he exposed himself from the fraudulent blanket of lies and faced the truth that he never left his room, touched a rail, or attended the funeral. Strength existed only in the prayers he said alone in his house eight miles from the cemetery he would not visit on the day of his brother's funeral.

Chapter 8
Failure

Sarah felt the waves of pain in an instant, like a bomb exploding inside her, when she saw him crying almost uncontrollably as she walked into his room. Despite all the tumbles, bruises, and tears, she faced raising her son, nothing could have prepared her for the motionless devastation sitting in the small room. Fifteen minutes passed since she returned home from the funeral and she reluctantly devoted that time to granting him his continued solitude. At last, she decided with wavering vehemence it had gone on for too long. He sat on his bed facing the window, turned away from his door and the world, holding his head in his hands. The quick up and down motions of his back were the only noticeable signs of his crying but those motions were clear, unmistakable. He did not change his position, or acknowledge her presence when his mother eased along side him and slid her comforting arm to his back. She already decided in her four steps across the room that she would force nothing from him. She simply knew, in the omniscient way mothers always know, she needed to be there. Leo knew too.

Echoing his repetitious query to God, a muffled "Why?" escaped between his sobs and between his hands to the sympathetic ears of his mother. Equipped with all the "Encyclopedia of Motherhood" answers, Sarah chose wisely to avoid them. "Everything happens for a reason", or "Walter is in a better place" would end the conversation immediately, badly. Instead, she reverted to every mother's first love, honesty.

"I don't know." She confessed the simplest ignorance that mirrored her son's and on the edge of the bed, on the darkest day, they understood one another. Time passed slowly while a mother and son sat silently in each other's arms. Together they comprehended the common denial among people who believe there is always something to be said. Sometimes there are no right words and there are no answers. Sometimes there are only tears, and in the best circumstances there are shoulders for them to fall upon.

Finally, Sarah gathered the strength to tell Leo what she hoped to avoid. She hung her head and found a safe spot in the dilapidated shag carpet. "Leo, I'm not sure if this is the right time, but there might never be a right time so I'm just going to tell you. I have some more bad news." She raised her head and steadied her gaze on her greatest love. "Are you ready to hear it?"

"Why not?" Leo's voice cracked sarcastically as he tried to gather himself for her benefit.

"I've got some news about your father." His attention grew as his mother began to explain.

On the afternoon Leo and Sarah embraced life and death, a man sat behind The Grand Hotel safely out of the view of the guests. He prepared for the inebriation that coexisted with his one night off. He sat on a cooler half full of Shlitz beer and looked out over the Atlantic considering his son who could be found in that direction. The forgiving sun warmed his back conveying the message that this day neared it's end. Richard knew the days ahead would be harder, and he enjoyed the idea. A dark pair of sunglasses shielded his eyes, and his tears, from the harsh reflections of the waning daylight on the water. The clutter of empty beer cans surrounding his feet made the usually serene atmosphere a bit pathetic. Richard Smith did in fact reek of alcohol, but the late afternoon beachcombers failed to realize in their snobbish glances at the misplaced man, that today started something new, something better.

Mr. Smith had a son, an ex-wife, an ex-mistress turned ex-girlfriend, and a slow monotonous job, but somewhere amidst the scrap pile, he looked to help. That same "why me?" that visits us all in our greatest moments of discontent, plagued Richard for a couple of torturous months. The southern bell stayed for years, but walked softly into the night more than a few weeks before the alcohol-induced contemplation of this afternoon. Richard could hardly hear the ringing in his ears, although it lasted longer then he initially suspected. He entertained the worst of his marvelous mood swings in those surreal weeks and remained tolerable through it all. Night watchman duty never required he serve as the poster child for courtesy and warmth; therefore, his job never gave him too much trouble.

Richard made a bad trade when he opted to release his family from the days of his discontent. Accepting the temptation of a different lifestyle felt easy when the waves broke over the beach on a night he would never forget, but as the thrill passed, and the reality of unhappiness crashed down around him, he began to miss his son and often times, the woman who left to raise him. While the term seemed inappropriate down to the deep recesses of his heart, he could not avoid the constant presence in his mind and the contrast it provided: *FAMILY*. Richard Smith knew that his life consisted of waiting for time to pass. No way to live.

"What do you think I should do?" Leo heard the whole story of his once removed father and the new drama. He understood drama never moved far out of Richard's reach, but remained unsure what they expected of him. "Leo, you need to make this decision on your own. I know, in fact everyone knows, you're going through a tough time right now. Maybe it could be good for you to get away for a while or maybe it's just too much too soon. I really don't know what would be best for you." Her deep sigh held back painful emotion. "Maybe you can figure it out."

"Maybe." Leo knew only that he could not make the decision in that room amid these circumstances. The trip could serve as a welcome escape from the pity and sympathy of those who would never know the whole story. The island might be a horror show of sequestered time where desolation and solitude became his best and only friends. He felt the normal fear accompanying the anticipation of starting over in a new place, but felt it coupled with the pain of the last few days and the terror of facing the consternation alone.

"Then again, if your father is in bad shape, things could be pretty tough on you. The last thing you need in your life right now is more problems. You've got a full load for yourself Leo. I'll stand by your decision, whatever it is, but it is your decision."

"I'm not sure I can decide."

"You have to." She rose from the bed and smoothed the wrinkles in the delicate comforter. The wrinkles did not disappear but she believed they would as the most difficult part of her day ended. She offered her son the chance to help his estranged father while simultaneously praying he would not go, knowing that he *must not* go.

"If I go, will you miss me?

"Always." From the doorway she made her last offer of the day conveying more comprehension than pity. "And, Leo, I'm sorry about Walter. I know you loved him…" Her words broke off, not with the innocence or ignorance of a person searching for the last phrase, but with the choked understanding and knowledge of the only phrase. She left the room without that last utterance, yet the emotion of the words filled the room. Amidst the confusion, in a way perhaps only mother's can, she chose the only path to her son: "like a brother." Leo knew the words all along, but tortured himself knowing he failed to say them.

Chapter 9
Leaving

The digital lights read *8:30* when he forced himself to sleep prepared for the demons to come, having accepted the exhaustion of his longest hours. He slept soundly until the first moments of dawn when he awakened to the penetrating stream of morning light, uninhibited by curtains pulled back the previous evening in a futile hope that answers would present themselves. Leo could recall only one dream in the course of the night and it revolved around the intrigue of Susan Watts. For that, he felt guilty. Consciously, he ignored any thought of her over the last three days. He briefly toyed with the notion that his subconscious fought to offer his mind a rest. He felt the need for none. In the four steps across the full length of his room to his infrequently dusted dresser he did not think of his guilty subconscious, he did not think of the pain unnecessarily shouldered by his mother, he did not think of saving his father. He thought of that silky smooth jumpshot, and nothing else, as he began to pack.

He used most of his strength to force a sweatshirt into the crowded darkness of his now bulging backpack. He looked across the room at the *Sports Illustrated Swimsuit Edition* on the nightstand next to his bed, and considered briefly that the ladies deserved a trip. Ultimately, he passed over Vendela and other models as quickly as he ever had, and decided against it. The calendar next to his bed warned him that three weeks of June already passed. If not for senior exemption, the thrills of an American Democracy final exam would occupy his mind. Thoughts of the exam made Leo realize that high school ended and he could never return to any part of the past, alone or not. He stood in the dim hallway again.

In two months, he would walk through the doors of a campus store and buy the necessary books for his first semester of college. He had two months to help his father find home, two months to miss his mother and the relationship of a lifetime, and two months to forget a spring evening with Susan Watts. Leo could not ignore the fraudulent effort he made to believe that he traveled to this island for any cause other than himself. He actually had eight weeks to attack, dissect, and examine the most important thing in his life. He went for one man. Leo Smith needed two months to convince himself that his friend knew with conviction, in the last breaths before his death, that his brother loved him. More than anything else he could ever wish for, Leo wanted back his best friend and brother. He knew the impossibility, so on a long road he would reluctantly settle for a few runs of stability. Of course, stability itself would never feel the same without the effortless friendship that carried him for so long.

The Fortun's knew and the Jeep readied for departure, accepting the weight of the load that consisted only of an Eastern Mountain Sports backpack, a green, eighteen-speed, Trek mountain bike, and two friends. The contents of the Jeep, like the vehicle itself, were battered and bruised from the years of harsh use and for the mother, son, bag, and bike, the journey began. Sarah and Leo fought minimal traffic on their way to a 9:30 a.m. ferry sailing out of New London and arriving in the reverse-anachronism known as Block Island. Few words were exchanged in the car and it suited them as they accepted with great clarity the unmistakable certainty that each of them could hardly breathe. The salty, morning smell of the river's mouth woke them from their haze of enabling fiction, as they turned left into the station and their suspension of belief continued to dissipate. Neither of them doubted his impending departure any longer.

Sarah and Leo stood less than ten feet from the ferry pondering what they could possibly say. The New London shore once served as a stomping ground for the wealthy, but long since fell ill with the disappearance of whaling. What once seemed to boom now only whimpered and those soft cries could be heard in the wind as a mother and son prepared to part. There, on the dock, love between friends rested in their eyes and for once they could accept a moment as traditional. Nothing ever seemed regular, or natural, in their turbulent relationship, but now, finally, they could do something all families do. They could do something with the care and concern of mothers and sons. They could say goodbye.

"Are you absolutely certain you want to do this?" Sarah asked the question nervously and her tone revealed her worry as greater than Leo's.

"No. I'm not absolutely certain of anything, but I think I can solve a lot of problems on this trip. I also think I might be in over my head." Leo paused, knowing he verged on doing something his mother never asked for, and never expected. He started to justify himself. "He may have been an asshole to you, but he is my father and he's never asked me for anything in my life."

"He's also never given you anything."

"Except my life." In an instantaneous flash that would have made the last hour much easier, Sarah understood Leo's reasons. "If I can help him we both know I should go. I've also got a lot to resolve before I take off for school. I have my own agenda." The statement felt strange to both of them because Leo rarely worked from his own agenda. "What about you? Do you think you'll be able to manage without all the aggravation I give you?"

"I'll try and manage." The sarcasm, clear as the day, could not have been missed. They lived with each other all his life and now life changed.

"Thanks for everything."

"What did I do?"

"I just told you." Leo turned and walked onto the boat, past the parked cars, and up the stairs leading to the main deck. An instant later a horn sounded and the ferry skulked out into the river. Slowly, the dock cleared of cars and workers until one woman stood alone. One thought entered the forefront of her mind slowly, but with raging clarity as the wake of the ferry had long since subsided. Sarah Parsons could not move from the rail of the dock, anchored by that single thought, so she held her body immobile while her mind raced. She was proud of her son.

Chapter 10
Grand

Leo confronted his anti-social personality early in life, understanding he would never be the life of the party or the salesman of the month. He would never laugh with tons of friends or spend an adolescent Friday afternoon charging toward the phone to find out about big weekend plans, and he understood what he missed. As the ferry coasted into the Old Harbor at Block Island, Leo stared apprehensively over the crowded streets into the never-ending stream of hotel windows and thought about solitude. In the midst of all the commotion, he finally stared into the face of the coming summer thinking this would be his time, his island, his place. He could not in his boldest efforts circumvent the nervous feeling that accompanied any thought of the next eight weeks.

Where the metal turned to wood Leo stepped off the end of the boat onto the dock and mumbled aloud, "Here we go." He readily remembered the rumblings of his father from earlier years and the warnings of his mother from the morning. The owners of The Grand Hotel were business people and the modern concerns of humanity were lost on them. The words warm and fuzzy meant nothing in their realm, and the trials of a young boy meant even less. Leo expected little help from them with the exception of room and board. Thoughts of his father continued to plague Leo, a man he had not seen in three years, and had not spoken to in over four months. As he fought through the crowded street toward the hotel, his mind suddenly focused solely on the fate of Richard Smith, a man he hardly knew. The additional plague burdening his mind proliferated itself in the form of one simple question. *How can I help?*

The construction of The Grand Hotel remains a blip on the screen in the mysterious history of supply and demand, where the temptation of the islands best corn muffins disguised less than luxurious accommodations. John and Maude Fortun brought every nickel they saved to the town of New Shoreham in 1930. 1930 was not a particularly good year for the world and independent wealth surfaced as a religion, which is to say it revealed itself most clearly as a belief or pursuit, rather than a common or tangible resource. John and Maude moved what remained of their tangible resources to the Block Island coastline forsaking their miserable Hartford, Connecticut existence that deflated them with Depression.

John procured a job on a small fishing trawler where blues and sea bass paid the rent. He loved the salty smell of the ocean and feared the open sea. In the years he spent on the ocean, he never truly gained his sea legs, but believed in earnest that the deep waters bellowed ageless stories, and he would one day find a surreptitious way to listen. Maude despised the ocean with a passion surpassed only by her hatred of the smell it left on her husband. When he no longer wreaked of hours at sea, his stench betrayed more than one chilly ale at the Block Island House, a Prohibition ale house filled with history, stories of fish "this big," and bottomless pints.

In 1933, the Block Island House would become the Block Island Pub, just as it was twelve years earlier. The House presented residents and tourists with a crystal reminder that not all the rules applied on the island, as they never would. Of course, there were police to enforce the laws and monitor the town, but they wasted no time with ridiculous ideas like outlawing alcohol. They had no time for the eighteenth amendment, no time for the Constitution. The boys loved their country, but when their backs were pushed to the wall, they were thirsty.

Aside from a beautiful view, and the clean, mind-clearing air, Maude's life moved one step closer to the warm side of purgatory. She left her friends, her family, and the grand parts of her life behind, consoling herself only with the undeniable certainty that she would always love the man she married.

1930 passed like a decade for Maude Fortun, but in the spring of 1931 she awakened to a bright, shining, light that entered the lives of the happy couple. John "Sticky" Wilson, a six-foot-three, one-hundred-and-fifty-pound fisherman, changed a small window of history in the Old Harbor. He arrived on the island without a care in the world or one thin dime in his pocket. He walked off the dock with the charisma of a small circus, straight into the Block Island House where he promptly sat down next to John Fortun. On a cool, dry, March day woven into the fabric of a meaningless conversation, The Grand Hotel took her first breath and she would forever change the lives of a young couple escaping the demons of the Great Depression. Sticky Wilson represented their first guest.

Sticky and John fought off sobriety, big fish tales, thoughts of empty glasses, and boredom, before they spoke of the glaring reality that Sticky knew no roof for the evening and John could offer a sofa. Maude Fortun thought Sticky Wilson was the end of the world when he arrived in her home that evening. That "rail of a man," as she called him the first evening, worked on a boat, drank in the house, and slept on her sofa for the next five weeks. Maude often complained to John about their "house guest," but her outbursts were always met by the same response: "He's no harm, Maude, and we can use the rent." Sometimes women cannot speak to men who love the ocean.

At the end of those five weeks, when the "rail of a man" and her husband began building the addition on her four-room cottage, Maude realized Sticky Wilson existed not as a boarder, but as an immovable and undeniable part of her life. John found comfort, Sticky found a home, and Maude, exhausting all her patience, found her sanity each morning as the crashing waves tried to tell her a story she refused to hear. The completion of the new addition came coupled with the proliferation of a new renter in the form of John "Pipes" O'Flannery. John O'Flannery moved in with John Wilson who lived with John and Maude Fortun.

Pipes O'Flannery earned his nickname by displaying the largest biceps any Block Island fisherman had ever seen. Rumor perpetuated the stories of Pipes pulling a one hundred and fifty pound fish out of the water and effortlessly escorting it onto the deck of the boat with one arm. The fisherman could not control their hysterical belly laughs when one of them mentioned Sticky's impending safety if he ever fell overboard.

Dinner for four became the nightly cottage ritual and rent for two paid weekly. Contrary to anything she could have expected, Maude reveled in the untimely arrival of Pipes. The additional rent allowed her a slightly better lifestyle, while a gentle-hearted man who mirrored Paul Bunion, warmed the house and served as a close friend to Sticky. That friendship gave her what she wanted more than anything; the full time husband she missed and still desperately loved. Slowly, a snowball began to roll on an open hillside adjacent to the Block Island Harbor, and the future of the exquisite, endless view seemed undeniable.

In 1934, Pipes O'Flannery fixed windows, chopped wood, collected rent, and occasionally broke up a late night rumble as the live-in, jack-of-all-trades at the twelve-room boarding house belonging to John and Maude Fortun. John Fortun still worked on a fishing boat with the relentless passion of a man who no longer needed the money. Sticky Wilson fell in love with a girl five years his younger in 1933 and promptly disappeared from the island. While disparity remained in the whispers of why he left, the many that loved him never forgot him. John liked to believe that Sticky traveled the world hoping his young love would never quite catch her breath. Pipes, a permanent pessimist, believed the more popular version that the seventeen-year-old girl divulged her unplanned pregnancy to her father who then chased the couple off the island. A photo of Sticky stood like a monument behind the bar of the Block Island Pub and John Fortun thought of him often. John Wilson, more than any man, changed his life, and his family, forever.

Maude Fortun took care of fourteen fishermen who emerged from the sea, the land, the pub, and her worst nightmares to become what she least expected: her sons and brothers. In addition to those fourteen lives, Maude watched most carefully over two others. In 1932, John and Maude were blessed with twin daughters who justified Maude's existence for the rest of her life, even into the depths of her last years in a place she never belonged.

By 1938, on the verge of the war to truly end all wars, only two fishermen remained in the company of the small hotel. Wealthy New England tourists sought the life created by Fitzgerald in 1925, even if they found it one week at a time. Not everyone received an invitation to Gatsby's parties, so other places emerged. A tasteful cottage with a splendid view of the Atlantic, and the best breakfast on the island, served as one of those elegant excursions. Pipes, now a practical artist framed the quaint cottage with a wrap-around porch decorating the structure like a cashmere shawl. On clear days he ignored the beauty of his work, squinted into the distance, and promised himself he could see John Wilson. Guests of the hotel could not see Sticky, or anything else, when they stared through the Martini haze into an ocean of improbability. The guests did not want to see; they embraced the cloudy days. On Block Island the rest of the world seemed incongruous, the unavoidable land war, now avoidable, women in factories felt incomprehensible, prohibition, now removed, never existed. There were soft sounds of jazz and the most beautiful views. The senses peaked for these artistic amenities and, of course, for the breakfast.

The war years were lean ones on the island and the shortage of men and tourists left empty rooms in the house of Fortun. The aged aristocrats still frequented the island, but very few could accept the modest accommodations of the not-yet-grand hotel. John Fortun finished many pints feeling remorseful he never fought in the war. He would have loved to serve his country in the navy, but all his years of offshore fishing never truly cured his fear of the open ocean, his second greatest love and his greatest fear. However, in trade for heroism, he earned a gift much greater. He watched his daughters grow up into young women, and ignoring all the trepidation that comes with daughters, he cherished each minute he spent with them.

By 1948, people began to feel safe again. That safety coupled with the booming economy changed the lives of the four Fortun's again. The twelve-room cottage underwent its fourth expansion, this time at the hands of professional contractors. When finished, the fifty-room Grand Hotel dominated the coastline as visitors scanned the harbor from incoming ferries. The Surf, The National, and The Grand sat like grandmothers waiting for their children to come home. Each year they did.

Maude and Margaret, took responsibility for the hotel in 1963, a task they trained for since their own adolescence. The island and the hotel were their true loves, which they proved by never marrying. As children, they sat in the comfort of their father's lap and begged with persuasive blue eyes to hear the story of Pipes and Sticky just one more time. The Grand became their child and they raised her well. In 1969, Maude Fortun died and in the following year an illness, which could only be described as heartache, took the life of John Fortun.

The front door of The Grand Hotel stood unopened before Leo like a Wells' novel. He traveled back in time when he broke the plane of the doorway and entered his own past. Memories of childhood began to flash through Leo's mind, but a remodeled lobby contrasted those thoughts. The wicker rockers once overcrowding the far corner of the room were gone, but his memories of countless hours in those chairs seemed fresher in their absence. In his fondest thoughts, he remembered the cool summer evenings when his father would bring him along on the night watch. Undeniably impressed by the vast emptiness of the hotel at night, Leo always insisted on staying awake through his father's watch, instead of returning to the cottage. The short debate was always followed by a long slumber in the cushions of the rockers. The cheap, pseudo-Victorian sofa now crouched in that same corner could never inspire a child's deep sleep with it's chipped edges and faded pleather cushions. The antique birdcage no longer cluttered the windowsill; the guest register, grandfather clock, and the chandelier, were also gone. In short, the mystique that awed the child vacated the room in recent years. In multiple ways, Leo was here on business.

Standing at the base of the curling stairway that extended to the first floor, he rang the bell at the front desk and looked back over the lobby so convincingly prepared for tourists. There were at least ten pictures on the walls of the moving of the Southeast Lighthouse. Leo remembered seeing pictures in newspapers and magazines of the countless people arriving to see the light. They did not come to see the beauty and tradition of the lighthouse standing, challenging the cliff as it withered away. They did not come to pay homage to the mass of bricks created by men to ensure the safety of other men. They simply came to see it move. Few people were impressed with the tradition that surrounded it or the architecture that made it. They were fascinated with the fact that men could move it. The priorities somehow seemed wrong, those pictures on the walls seemed wrong, and the rack of T-shirts for sale behind the front desk bothered Leo as well. He knew there existed a place for memories of that island. Maybe a place in someone's heart, or someone's mind, a journal, anything! The island encapsulated on a T-shirt could never serve as a souvenir of the heart. They did not belong. Lost in thought, as he stared at the shirts, he failed to notice Maude Fortun walk into the room.

"Those shirts are lovely aren't they?" Her voice jolted Leo out of his trance and he turned his attention to her. More than six years had passed since Leo last saw her, and now deep into her sixties, she looked closer to eighty. Fifty years of running after small children who entered the hotel neglecting to wash their feet took its toll.

"Miss Fortun?" he asked inquisitively, even though he never forgot the face etched into his earliest years.

"Yes, can I help you with something." Her voice had changed slightly in the recent years and Leo thought maybe some of the industrious businesswoman disappeared. He thought he observed a faint touch of a more favorable "sweet old lady." Leo could ponder this thought along with many others in the coming weeks of uncertainty, but currently the lobby demanded a more pressing thought; introductions.

"I think you've been expecting me. I'm Leo Smith." Miss Fortun's reaction tore a path through the wrinkles and appeared clearly on her face. She expected Leo to walk through the door, but she expected a child, not the man in front of her. A gray cloud of disbelief filled her eyes when she began to focus on a face she had known but forgotten.

"It doesn't seem possible, Leo. I'm looking at the man before me and straining to see the child who left this island." She could have stared for days without finding the child's eyes that still existed two weeks ago. That child's face now hardened in the wake of despair, an unforgivable sin. The curves of his face sharpened; the eyes darkened and his face showed loss; not loss of weight, or color; nothing that simple. His face defined a loss of clarity. He stood before her as a child recovering from a man size loss.

"I guess the child is fading."

"Let's hope he hasn't gone far. How was your trip? The ferry ride didn't give you any trouble did it? The waters look a little rough today." Years passed since Leo made that ride, but Miss Fortun immediately remembered how he always loved the trip to the distant mainland. When his father took day trips for the family, or the hotel, Leo always insisted on going with him. He would stand close to the ship's rail and wonder about the chaos of life existing below. Occasionally, he envisioned himself as the captain of a submarine, or the commander of a battleship planning an ambush, outsmarting the enemy. Sometimes he just wished for scuba gear and his father's permission to dive over the side into the calm, deep blue. The wonder of possibility drove that child to the edge, but on this afternoon he rode inside the ship. He never even looked out a window.

"The trip was fine. If you could just show me where to put my things I wouldn't mind resting for a while."

"Well, I'd love it if you could tell me a bit about how life has been for you and your mother." Her genuine concern surprised Leo.

"Maybe we can talk a little later." Maude Fortun observed enough life to understand the intricacies and subtleties of the sad young man in the lobby of her hotel. With more than fifty years of emotion in the room, she knew the conversation could wait. Leo needed rest, not for hours but for days, maybe months, so she would not push the issue. "We've cleared out the bottom floor of the cottage for you. It's been vacant since your father moved out and we thought you might want to revisit the old home. I've got a few things to do, do you remember the way?"

"Yes."

"The keys are in the same place." Leo could feel the hint of a breeze at his back as a tired woman made her way toward the hotel's kitchen. It seemed as if the breeze came up simply to aid her along the way. Leo looked behind him through the lobby's closed windows out into the street, where he saw the scrambling tourists marching on toward the next souvenir shop. He turned again and headed through the empty lobby toward the back door. He walked alone again and for that one thing he became incredibly thankful.

The seven years he missed were a speck in time in the considerable fifty-year history of the Grand Hotel. Imitation gold frames surrounded the images of the ghosts of Christmas past. The old patrons of The Grand captured time and time again, and displayed before the self-absorbed newcomers. The ideas that built the hotel remained solely with those who originally understood it. The Victorian era was not dead in the eyes of the building, only slumbering in the midst of hibernation, sheltered from the presence of those who stretched on in quest of an "I Rocked on the Block" T-shirt.

The black and white photos showed the stern faces and strong backs of those who labored at The Grand of years past. Waiters in wool suits posed with the serving women in full-length gowns. The padded shoulders climbed past New England Patriots and reached for a higher place where sanctity lived as more than a word. Their shoulders stretched for tin ceilings that still hooded the top of the lobby and dining room. The original tins failed to stand the test in all the rooms, but on that floor a piece of estranged architectural history clung like determined vines. The bookshelves stretched from the carpets, past the shoulders, up toward the ceilings, but not quite that far. The gold leafed volumes adorning the shelves were to be looked at, not read; a sad end for so many torrid tales. Many times hotel patrons would gather in the old days to hear the one guest, a bit more vociferous than most, who would test his lungs and tell a tale. Always a brave man; quite a shame for some tales. The time warp lacked some omnipotent picture hanging high above the oak front desk to remind the new patrons of the history of their grand stay. The picture would never sell because no one would buy it, and anyone could paint it. The beauty of that picture lies only with those who can understand it. Perhaps a portrait of Sticky Wilson would do, perhaps not. Ultimately, nothing can really keep the times from changing.

Leo stumbled out the back door in a state of confusion. He knew the direction, and certainly how to get there, yet the path was discrete. He felt lost in the passage of time erupting through the cracks of the walk with each step into a life that belonged somewhere long behind him. He staggered toward the cottage, focused on the crashing waves of the ocean, rather than the crashing ideas wandering across his newfound life. For a moment, everything seemed all right and he knew the next breath had to be negative. He inhaled.

Pushing open the cottage door caused another small cut in the curve of the space-time continuum and Leo took one more step toward his childhood. He stepped back into a time that deserted him long ago; a time almost erased from his memory. Childhood should have reached up from the melancholy corners of the hall and lunged toward him, but instead it paused waiting for the hour when it's owner would be prepared. The color of the walls and smell of the hall were as dulled as the memories of the new guest. Excitement crept away on the back of the small, lethargic, beetle moving toward the corner.

The newest member of The Grand Hotel staff meandered down the hall without empathy for a place that no longer existed. The home his parents made not long ago, weathered in sync with their past marriage, and both now converged while leaving him alone. Leo pushed open the door to his new bedroom. The quiet movement of the door amplified the creak he expected to hear. Large, luxurious, and spacious were adjectives lost on a room that cried out for a friend. With the bed carefully made, and the room partially cleaned, a young man on a journey gambled with his most impressive move yet: he fell and slept, soundly.

Leo awoke when a strong hand shook him slightly. Looking up through glazed eyes, he wondered for a second where he slept and who now towered over him. Focusing on the bland wall came easier than recognizing the face not seen in three lost years. Until he heard the voice and put the two together, he could not experience absolute certainty.

"Listen, I'm awful sorry I didn't meet you at the boat, but I got held up. You look good. Why don't you take a shower and meet me across the street for a beer. There's a place called O'Mally's. You can't miss it." As quietly as he entered, the man Leo strained to remember walked out the door. Richard Smith, his father, had just invited his seventeen-year-old son for a beer.

Leo strained to imagine those brief words as reality. The idea of dreaming of his father entering the room and offering O'Mally's seemed much more plausible. He wrestled away the thoughts that his father actually surpassed the disgusting man his mother described. Not one single meaningful word came out of the man's mouth. Leo scanned the room closely for the first time and found the clock: 1:25. "Meet me across the street for a beer." He really said it.

Freshly showered, Leo meandered through the dining room of the hotel unable to shake the Hallmark beginning with his father. "Did you see him?" Maude Fortun's voice called out from the kitchen.

"Very briefly."

"O'Mally's?"

"O'Mally's."

"Good luck, Leo."

"You've said that already."

"I know. You're going to need a lot of it." Her face appeared in the doorway to offer her last sentiment and her smile showed less sympathy than understanding when she offered her honest appraisal of the paternal conflict. She seemed to provide confidence rather than acknowledge Leo had none.

"Wonderful." Leo pointed out the front door. "This way?"

"Can't miss it."

"Thanks."

Richard Smith failed to appear when his son entered the pub called O'Mally's, pitched his ID on the counter, and ordered, "Beer. Large."

The bartender carefully looked over the Ohio driver's license Leo Smith purchased on a road trip to Boston. "Sure thing Mr. Richardson." The sarcasm flowed much thicker than the lager she poured. The attractive woman behind the bar obviously cared very little about serving the fraudulent Mark Richardson. The twenty-three-year-old server concerned herself only with the pouring of Samuel Adams.

"Busy place." Leo forced down some of the first beer he ordered in his entire life.

"It can be. Once the sun sets every loud mouth, know-it-all, cocky moron on this island, who can consume more than fifteen beers, walks through that door."

"What a coincidence." Leo laughed at the matching description.

"How's that?"

"I think I'm looking for their leader. Do you happen to know a guy named Richard Smith?"

The bartender continued to prepare for the inexorable crowd that appeared nightly without fail and answered Leo as if she were talking to someone else. "I know a lot of faces but not many names." She pulled two bottles of cheap rum from under the counter behind the bar and placed them in the well. "For example, I have no idea who this Mark Richardson guy is. Do you?" With the question, she finally directed a glance at Leo.

"I'm not sure I understand."

"I'm trying to explain that sometimes it's hard to put the names with the faces. You've been in here for less than five minutes and I've seen two faces and only one name. I'm certain one of the three belongs to you." She paused allowing Leo to squirm behind his pint then released him from his embarrassment. "I guess what I really wanted to say is that it's very nice to meet you, Mark." She extended her hand over the chipped mahogany, past the brass rail, and offered it to Leo. Unaware of what would follow, Leo extended his arm to meet her handshake. "I'm Lady Megan, Queen of Block Island.

Leo pulled his hand back and struggled to find a far off place called dignity. "Well, if you don't believe me maybe I should take my business elsewhere." As the words escaped, Leo realized his bravado act paralleled the worst thespians of daytime television.

"Don't sweat it, kid, your secret is safe with me. You look the part. It's your ID that fails you. Besides I can't let you leave. You're too cute. Just for the record my name is actually Megan, and if I seem a little bitchy it's because I work in this place about sixty-five hours a week and hate dealing with the wall to wall knuckleheads who patronize us."

Distracted by fake identification and thoughts of his father, Leo previously failed to notice the subtle beauty of the facetious woman pouring drinks. She would never emerge from behind the scenes onto a Paris runway and an Ivory soap advertisement would be a stretch, but she allowed Leo the one moment of rest he needed. Across the bar, he forgot his father, he ignored his matchbox living quarters, and he failed to listen as Megan finished her sentence. His mind shut out the enigmatic world, while carbonation bubbles floated upward and he pondered the intentions of the phrase "too cute." Finally the tranquillity in his mind broke, interrupted by the sound of a dead man walking.

"Megan, you taking care of this boy?" The muffled question surfaced from behind him, but surprisingly, Leo now recognized the voice of his father immediately. He allowed himself only a quick glance over his shoulder where he spotted the aging, weathered man who invited his teenage son for a beer. Leo turned back toward the bar.

"You really were looking for their leader," Megan confided in Leo before Richard reached his son's side. Her voice comforted him like the safety of a crossing guard, appearing only to interrupt the oncoming traffic of Mr. Smith. She stepped back to the curb and let the traffic pass. "You bet, Mr. Smith. You know I take care of everyone."

"Well, well, well. How's my boy doing?" Richard smelled of alcohol and would have benefited from a shave. Leo continued to fix his gaze on Megan nodding in ascension at her questioning countenance.

"Not so well." Leo, unprepared for small talk, broached the topic concerning him most on the first day of his tempestuous trip. "Why would you ask your seventeen-year-old son, who you haven't seen in years, to meet you in a bar? Did it just seem like the perfect morning for a beer?" Leo did not pause to ponder when he became so furious.

"It's past noon."

"Barely."

"I just figured if we were going to have a father-son conversation I'd probably need a drink."

This angered Leo further as despair once again took hold of all his strongest emotions. "What you need is a sharp razor and a whole roll of Lifesavers." Megan allowed a brief laugh to escape but turned away before Richard could catch her eyes.

Richard prepared himself for Leo's reaction, he expected the hatred, he understood the anger, but he never predicted the sharp pains controlling his body with each of his son's hostile words. A giant lump formed in a throat once impervious to sadness and a father said nothing in response to his unforgiving son. The father who cheated, lied, deceived, and finally slipped out his boy's life fell forward into the arms of his son.

From his first bar stool Leo hesitantly embraced incredulity and his estranged father in the same motion. Words followed slowly. “Why don’t we find someplace where we can talk.” Leo paused, waiting for whatever effort would come from the morose man he hated and loved for so many disappointing years. Richard said nothing when he released himself from Leo’s surprisingly strong arms. He turned slowly then walked across the room and out the door. Leo left a five-dollar bill on the bar and left without another glance toward Megan.

Two men walked out of O’Mally’s pub leaving behind a dark, sympathetic mahogany bar, an overused Guinness dart board, lonely cold draughts, and most surprisingly, a welling tear in the eye of a puzzled bartender intrigued by her newest customer.

Richard and Leo sat on the last few boulders of the jetty that separated the ocean from the harbor. Seaweed climbed high on the rocks exposed from the short water of low tide and the delicate spray from the tiny struggling waves lacked the power to reach the two silent men. The sounds of the placid sea and the cool wind broke the otherwise merciless heat but went unnoticed as these men challenged each other without words or movement. Finally, usurping the long-relinquished role of father, Richard broke the silence in time with the timid waves. “Why does this have to be so hard?”

“Sarah Parsons.” His response arrived without a nanosecond of thought revealing predetermined ideas. The ocean scene collapsed in behind Leo until Richard could see only the heated glaze over the boy’s eyes and the look of hatred projected toward him. “That is why this has to be so hard.”

“I definitely could use a drink.”

“That’s the rumor.”

“Maybe this was a bad idea, Leo.” For the first time, he realized that his son had been hardened by his own actions.

His mistakes were magnified within a young man who long ago discarded the idea of being a father's son.

"If not now, when?"

"Maybe never."

"So that's it? I've interrupted your drinking and the conversation is over. Or is it your conscience? All those screw-ups coming back to haunt you, so you're out. No chance. This discussion isn't over until you finally understand what you took from me."

"Leo, I left you and your mother a long time ago. What could I have possibly taken from you that you don't already have back?" When he finished the sentence and saw the macabre look on Leo's face, he wished only that he never asked. Awaiting the unavoidable maelstrom, Richard took a deep breath.

"A life." Leo paused, only for a moment, to notice the ocean surrounding him for the first time. "You took a life I can never have back again. There are no keys to open the doors of the places I need to go. No magical passport back to that life. The life you took is gone. It's dead and buried. A life was lost and I can't ever have it again. You're the one who closed the doors. You slammed every one in my face. I can't beg or plead, run or hide, or talk myself back to that place. It's gone." Richard raised his hand to Leo as he thought he saw a second of weakness in the boy's face. No such second ever existed. "I'm not you though, and I'll always have that to be thankful for. I can't close the door the way you did, I'll never fall where you fell, and that trap will never get me. In the end, I'll help you the way you couldn't help me. When that's done, this conversation is over, and maybe a new one can begin."

Richard Smith sat stagnant, alone with his contorted vision of the day. "Leo I..."

Leo cut off his father's feeble attempt and exploded calmly, as if he were clearing his throat. "You took my childhood, you son-of-a-bitch." His gaze dropped with his words until he could see the boulders supporting them both over the ocean. When he lifted his eyes, he turned away from his father and stared toward something over the horizon. He did not stare at the ocean, or the sky or the end of the earth. He focused on something much further away. "I'll start the night watch tonight. I'll find you when I'm ready to talk again."

Richard contemplated a few words, but finally made the crucial and necessary decision to leave. He failed his son, as he failed himself and he contemplated this day, feeling that like his own life, it was a terminal case. When his shoes sunk into the soft sand of the beach, he turned back toward his powerful son sitting on the jetty who now looked less like a boy on the rocks and more like part of them. Richard could not avoid the inevitable truth that in the course of their conversation, Leo never flinched. His words exploded like thunder in Richard's ears, but the young man actually showed no sign of emotion, no feeling, no caring and never once looked as if he would cry. The last thought scared Richard the most as his lachrymal glands detonated and tears raced down his cheeks wetting the sand below.

Chapter 11
Emerson

"Harboring your thoughts?" The voice sounded from behind Leo, clearly directed toward him, but he never moved. "Yeah, that's the good thing about these rocks. A sequestered man journeys out here and soon enough, he'll forget the whole world. Of course, I guess for some folks that can be both good and bad. It can be real tough to move forward alone if you're dragging someone else's stuff along behind you. I believe it was Emerson who said, 'The only thing grief has taught me, is to know how shallow it is.' You know what I mean?"

Leo heard no answer behind him. Turning his head he humored the man, "Are you talking to me?"

"I certainly hope so. Otherwise I'm speaking in soliloquy and that can be a real dangerous thing for a man to do, if you know your Shakespeare. Internal thought aloud for an audience is damaging enough, but it's more likely madness if no one is listening."

The man standing behind Leo looked a little bit lost and found at the same time. The sun ceaselessly curled down from its overhead perch, fading to the west, and supporting the background for a man who spoke of soliloquy and solitude. A full, untamed, graying beard nearly covered his mouth, which contorted to form shades of a Southern accent escaping through each word he spoke. His faded blue jeans carried a color most similar to brown, the result of both sun and soil. His flannel shirt flaunted itself, defying the weather forecast, making an appearance two months past the date when it should have been closeted for the season. The words "A" "HI" could be read on his tee shirt in two rows between the unrestricted flow of the unbuttoned flannel. The mood changed for those with a keen eye when a breeze opened the button-down revealing the secret message: "EAT SHIT." Dark glasses covered his eyes leaving his face incapable of expression.

Leo studied the new face before him wishing one of two things would happen; either the man would turn and head home quickly for a shower, or the wind would shift. The gentleman smelled of nature as a fishing boat does. Suddenly, without any evidence of physical exertion the man's body turned back toward the beach. With the ease of this simple movement he appeared to be floating rather than standing. He leaned his forehead back, letting his long twisted locks fall behind him and stared into the serene blue of the sky. "Yes. I do love this place." Leo failed to discern whether "this place" referred to the wall, the island, or the earth itself. The man continued to look skyward as he walked off toward the beach with a powerful conviction Leo could describe with one word: ownership. The transient man he observed moved along the rocks staring toward the sun and the sky as if they belonged to him. In the final confusion, Leo thought he heard the echo of two words released by the man, deflected off the ocean. "They do."

When the bells of the modern wall clock in the lobby finally struck ten, Leo wandered, seemingly aimless, but with a purpose, from the cottage to the hotel. He maneuvered down the well-lit path between the bushes, along the fence, toward the hotel nearly one hundred yards ahead. Unlike his morning trip down the path in the other direction, Leo now wished he could look out to the ocean, but even where the bushes thinned he could not see through the dark night and the gaunt fog. He could hear the waves crashing as before, and for now that would suffice as his glimpse of the Atlantic. Mentally he struggled, pondering solutions to his father's "hard luck," but his mind deceived his concentration, overwrought with thoughts of Walter. He did not sleep well during his fleeting afternoon nap and he knew a long night had just begun.

With a sudden push of energy in his stride, random thoughts reverted back to the last time he gave up a night's sleep. He and his best friend weaseled out of their houses armed only with a basketball and twelve beers. On the rarest occasions his friend would swindle a few beers from his mother's "in case of guests stash" and the exceptional boys would be normal. The plan was to play ball, drink beer, and see a sunrise. They would stroll home early and unnoticed.

"What will you do when your mom drives right on into the park and drags you home like the old days?"

"I'd just tell her I was down here practicing for college."

"And what about the beer, Week?"

"That's what I meant." Leo could not stop his laughter.

"I didn't realize they drank beer at Princeton."

"They will when I get there."

"Tell me brother, do all you black guys want to change the world." The simple, spectacular smile, rather than words, answered the last question. Leo smiled back knowing that in a battle of wits, like basketball, he typically found himself out-manned.

The two stayed in the park for more than four hours that night playing basketball, drinking Old Milwaukee, and talking about life in ways young men rarely do. For them "life" consisted mostly of basketball, the future, and each other. With eager prompting, the conversation occasionally included, or at least brushed on, racism or politics, and they found their views to be more similar than different. Leo considered himself an idealist more than an optimist and loved the skeptical counterpoint that remained omnipresent in good company. Leo believed any problem could be solved with enough time and effort and hoped he would not prove himself wrong when he arrived at the matter of Richard Smith.

"Hello, Miss Fortun," Leo said as he walked in the back door of the hotel. The elder Margaret Fortun stood on a chair in the center of the lobby watering a plant hanging from a small hook in the tin. She made no effort to conceal her look of surprise when she turned carefully, and her eyes found Leo. Like any person who sees time as an asset, she skipped the pleasantries. "I understand you saw your father today. Can I assume that all went well with the two of you. Well, I mean your still here. That's good, isn't it?"

"I'd rather not speak too soon. I'm not so sure Richard and I are eye to eye on the reason I'm here."

"So we'll just say you're here for now. That much certainly is true." The elderly woman turned her back to Leo, continuing her late evening watering as the door to the dining room opened and Maude Fortun stepped into the lobby. Unyielding to God's will, she moved as a woman twenty years younger. She immediately acknowledged Leo this time and extended her arms as she moved through the room. She squeezed Leo like a lost relative transferring a small feeling of hope from herself to him. "It's amazing how he's grown, isn't it Margaret?" Margaret continued watering knowing her sister's rhetoric. "Are you ready to start? Do you have any questions? Is there anything you need?" The series of rapid-fire questions startled Leo, but he sifted through and offered his one global concern.

"Maybe you could explain to me exactly what it is I'm going to be watching." Not renowned for its criminal element, the town of New Shoreham never prided itself on impenetrable security. The three island police officers encountered more trouble keeping drunks off the street than keeping hotels safe, and most homeowners locked their doors for the winter and nothing else.

"Margaret is the professional around here. Maybe she should explain." Maude Fortun strolled past Leo and attacked the stairs two at a time exiting the room. Margaret never ceased watering to offer her brief explanation. "It's really quite simple Leo. Just make sure everyone is out of the lobby by one o'clock and then lock the doors. Once everyone is gone, you turn off the lights in the lobby, but not on the porch. If no one comes along banging on the front door or the windows, the thing you watch most is television. Every once in a while you should take a walk upstairs just to make sure nothing strange is happening. Other than that just try not to go to sleep." Confronted with both happiness and fear, he heard the answers he expected. The tranquillity could be his best friend or it could leave him overwhelmed with thoughts of his best friend. People always wish for time to sort things out, but often end up lost in that time.

The rookie night watchman closely observed the clocks and the passing of 1:00 a.m. on his first tour of duty. The doors were locked and a lone figure sat cradled safely in the arms of a chair swing on the front porch of The Grand Hotel. Just after 3:00 a.m., the sound of a door slamming shut across the street woke him from the sleep Margaret Fortun warned him against. Through his glazed eyes, he saw the shadow of a figure on the opposite sidewalk coming toward him. Having no idea that an hour passed him in his slumber, he assumed he witnessed a late straggler escaping O'Mally's in a last call stagger.

"Is that you?" The unknown person called out to him through the darkness.

Certain the straggler spoke to him across the empty street he responded. "It's definitely me, but who are you looking for?"

"Oh my god, it's not Richard. It's Richardson." Leo failed to make that connection before. "What the hell are you doing over there? Sleeping?"

His groggy eyes still failed to make the simple recognition but his ears did not miss the condescending cue. "With one eye open."

"Where's Richard?"

"Bartender Megan, it's a long story." She walked across the street, stood on the cement sidewalk fronting the hotel, and leaned against the railing of the porch. Only a few feet now separated the two strangers.

"Well, you know my name but I'm not quite sure what to call you unless you're willing to accept 'Mack' outside the bar room as well." She smiled cautiously at Leo's obvious embarrassment.

"That's Mark by the way. And it's actually Smith, as in son of Richard Smith. The gentleman you're looking for has been indefinitely relieved of his nightly duties." Not a note of sadness could be heard in his voice as he spoke cautiously into the night.

"I'm not here looking for Richard." Megan could here the disgust in her voice betraying a thought she never meant to divulge. "I just know he works the watch at The Grand because he complains about it every night when he leaves O'Mally's at 10:15. Like clockwork, just when the crowd starts filling the bar, he staggers across the street toward this old place, but I'm certain I've never seen him out on the porch before."

"Never?" This time, Leo's words betrayed him but Megan could not have known that Leo's surprise stemmed from memories of a young boy rocking to sleep with his father on this very same porch.

"Never."

"I wonder if anything is the same as it used to be." Megan did not respond. Clearly, Leo's search for answers swelled within his own mind and her only outlet involved a change in the subject.

"So what are you doing here?"

"If you promise to be a little more direct maybe I'll answer."

Megan showed her own embarrassment for the first time since meeting the son of Richard Smith. "I'm sorry. I didn't mean to pry. I just don't have enough time to be polite when the look on your face tells me a trip to see dear old Dad isn't vacation for you." She paused, waiting for the agreement he would not offer. "You've got an agenda."

"What else is in your crystal ball?"

"What are you looking for?"

Caught off guard by another direct volley, Leo failed to fashion a clever response. His eyes locked onto Megan without looking at her. She noticed his arduous stare and felt helplessly alone in his presence. He paused for only a moment, before the one word answer seeped quietly through his lips. "Forgiveness."

The expression on the bartender's face changed and the involuntary shift exposed new sentiment with the comprehension that she listened to a young man in pain. She could clearly define the five or six years that separated them until the instant when Leo leered at her through a single, solitary word. Then the years disappeared.

"Are you waiting to forgive him or is he waiting to forgive you?" Megan hardly noticed her prying into the life of a stranger and proceeded with her questions never showing any particular concern for the general rules of politeness or privacy. If Mark Richardson-Smith wanted her to walk away he would simply ask, and with complete brevity, the conversation would end. If he commented on her lack of discretion she would surely forgive herself. If she never asked, she would not.

"Neither."

Megan broke the tension, endeavoring toward much needed comic relief, and hoping to ease the apprehension of her new friend. "You know if you gained forty pounds and ducked a razor for a few weeks you'd look just like him."

"Very flattering."

"Just an observation," Megan smiled. "Can I assume you don't know too many people around here?"

Leo held up the five fingers on his left hand while letting his head fall against the back of the chair swing, feigning interest in the ceiling of the porch. "The owners of the hotel, my father, and you."

"That's only four math whiz."

"The last person belongs on this island about as much as I do. A puzzle. No name, invisible face, but a strong odor I will remember for the rest of my peaceful days. If I smell him, I'll know him." Leo let out an unemotional sigh.

"Are you really this strange?"

"Another long story, but for the most part, no not at all. It's a pleasure to meet you again." Leo extended his hand out over the railing without dropping his gaze from the dark porch ceiling.

"It's nice to meet you too," Megan replied as she reached for his outstretched hand.

"So, young Mr. Smith, why don't you come by O'Mally's tomorrow at about eleven and I'll present you with the not so famous, bartender-guided tour of our little Block." She assumed he would agree and proceeded without a response. "The best way to see all the sights is by bike. Do you have one?"

"I'll build one." Intrigued by the offer, Leo contained his surprise, while entertaining the idea of patting himself on the back for his witty response.

"See you at eleven." Megan released his hand and started to move away.

"Hey, Megan, do you have a last name?

"Hey, Smith, do you have a first one? I'll see you tomorrow."

Relaxed and fearful, Leo sat for nearly ten minutes and asked himself questions. "Who is she?" "Why would she take me on a tour of the island?" He slid off the aging wooden swing and entered the lobby bothered by his natural instinct to question himself while walking toward the stairs. Every sane person wonders with whom he is speaking during elaborate sessions of thinking aloud, and why he chooses to speak to no one at all. For Leo this external self-questioning remained constant. Always bothered by the incessant flow of questions he forced on himself, he thought back to the transient man on the breakwall. *A sign of madness*? For Leo, the verbal observations represented a regular necessity rather than madness. Evaluation through questioning remained as a continuing self-reliance therapy. Emerson.

He stood in the first floor hallway with his thoughts rearranged and he found himself alone in a frightening sunlit alleyway. "Why did he have to die?" The unavoidable question. His mind twisted violently and brought him back to the quiet void of a lost street in New York. Forgiveness. Emotion exposed, Leo began to beg, from a Victorian hallway, for the chance to say goodbye. His equilibrium gave way and the wall slid underneath him, supporting his physical and mental weakness. In the wake of a useless day,

Leo felt his deepest stabs of pain. He knew he could help the father he rarely thought of, he could endure the solitude of the island, he could work the late hours, but at the end of the labyrinth, despair would close the gate. He could not solve the misery of losing his best friend. When the journey ended Leo would always see the scared eyes of an eighteen-year-old boy who never expected the end. He remained at the top of the curling hallway steps, amidst the silence of The Grand lady for the next hour staring into his distant and recent history, but most of all, into those eyes.

"You heard me, asshole." The escalated voice on the street saved Leo from an oncoming slumber waiting patiently for a 4:30 a.m. attack. "Keep your goddamned hands off me." Leo moved to the window and strained to see past the lobby's ostentatious reflection and out into the street. The silhouettes of the caustic woman and the menacing man following moved along Main Street past the hotel in the direction of the beach.

Without warning, the woman made a quick one hundred and eighty-degree turn facilitating a confrontational pose. In a single harmonious motion, the turn delivered an open fist that connected solidly with the man's unsuspecting face. *Bullseye.* The woman knocked him back a step, but only a step. Leo moved.

Grabbing the woman by her flailing arms, the man easily controlled her attack and pushed her into the shadows of the *Island Gift Shop*. When Leo approached, he could see the man warning the woman for the slap, rather than threatening any physical harm. He appeared drunk more than dangerous, and that helped to calm Leo as he disrupted the dispute.

"What seems to be the problem here, folks?" As the words escaped his mouth, Leo realized the Keystone cops could have taught him a thing or two about intimidation. He stood only a step away from the drunken couple, who failed to see him approach. When the drunkard turned and faced him completely, Leo's stomach sank in a momentary pause before his fist landed squarely in the center of the man's face. The man fell to the ground in a motion as fluid as the furious punch which put him there.

"Holy shit," the woman gasped.

"Go home," Leo responded, as remorse replaced anger, for the instantaneous action he never should have taken.

"Shouldn't we call the police or something? I mean don't we have to report him?"

"Could you do me a favor, lady, and please just go home and forget this happened. Believe me, this guy will never bother you or any other woman again." Leo looked at the unconscious figure on the ground and noticed the blood thinned by alcohol, flowing profusely from his nose. "Please!"

"All right. I guess I should trust you. I hope you're right." The woman calmly turned and walked away expressing no further concern, fear or anger. The paradoxical event puzzled Leo but the thought passed quickly as he leaned back to the forthcoming task.

Richard Smith looked pathetic, a passed out heap of flesh three paces from the Main Street sidewalk. Leo knew the alcohol, rather than the blow he delivered, perpetuated Richard's nap so he refused to worry about the health of the man he arrived here to help. Leo laughed, thinking that altruism rarely begins with a right hook. Left with the difficult task of moving a one-hundred-ninety-pound man from the fetal position to his own shoulder, Leo shook his head and continued to smile, not for the sake of humor, but for every child who ever felt ashamed of his parents. He grabbed his father, under both arms, lifting him to a standing position, and hoisting him onto his shoulder. Approaching the cottage, Leo once again listened closely to the sound of the ocean under the sound of his own deep breaths, and wondered what his father would remember in the morning.

After safely depositing his father on the floor of his extravagant living quarters, Leo returned to the hotel lobby where he found Margaret Fortun waiting by the registration desk. "Any problems, Leo?"

"Just checking the grounds."

"When I came out to the desk and saw you weren't here, I figured maybe we'd lost you."

Leo chose to avoid any further discussion regarding his whereabouts or the chaos caused by his father, so he shifted the conversation to the present. "What are you doing up so early anyway?" His suddenly gentle voice split the air and a tone of youthful concern surrounded Leo's question.

"Well to be honest, your father hasn't been a very reliable night watchman as of late and I've tried to keep one eye open. I guess it's a disadvantage of sleeping in the hotel." She paused, hesitant to reveal a deeper and more personal thought. "I guess it's my own little version of sleeping with my love." The hardened woman uttered the sentence as if speaking to the lobby rather than the young man in front of her.

"Any excitement tonight?" Now Margaret chose to change the subject.

"Nothing unusual," Not knowing exactly what *the usual* meant, Leo smiled the way a man does when he owns sacred information.

"Would you like a cup of coffee before you go?"

"I'd like a blanket and a pillow."

"Sleep tight, Leo."

"I will." Leo paused after two steps and examined the old woman as she moved away from him through the lobby. He witnessed a rare form of strength reserved only for those who believe in protecting their love. "You might want to try it yourself sometime," Leo whispered acknowledging her constitutions.

Leo returned to his room in the dilapidated cottage where he found Richard sound asleep in the comfort of his bed and as promised, Leo continued the fight against his father's demons. Like an inept magician, Leo pulled the covers out from underneath his father, who slid like a fragile vase, until he met the floor with a resounding *thump*. The crash could have awoken the dead, along with many of the guests in the ocean side rooms, but did not wake the drunk. Leo kicked his father a few times as if he were checking a tire for air, but the alchemistic alcohol continued to win the raging battle against the pain. The resolute young man smiled contentedly at his father on the wooden floor. "I see we've opted for the long term plan." Naturally, there were no short-term solutions for allowing the merciful bottle to slip from one's hand, but Leo, in his youth, hoped to find such an answer. He fired his only pillow at his father who began to snore, and laid down in defeat losing his own battle against exhaustion. Richard, seemingly unaware of the world, or his son's attack, rolled onto the pillow comforting his head from the cold, adamantine floor.

Thirty minutes later convinced his son slept soundly, Richard stood up, relieving some mild back pain incurred from his fall on Main Street, and walked cautiously toward the door. He turned off the light and fought off regret as he mouthed three words across the dark room. "Good night, son." He walked through the deserted parking lot and allowed the tears to flow freely for the second time in sixteen hours, and the third time in his entire life.

Chapter 12
Megan

When Leo awoke, confronted by the clock that flashed 10:50, he entertained no visions of the previous night or any of the memories created. He thought of more sleep and the wondrous possibilities for the irresponsible. With his best legerdemain, he convinced himself that none of the horrors were real, until he rolled to the edge of the bed and remembered a floor no longer occupied. The sun pierced through the hole in the drab window shade and warned Leo again of late morning. He shifted his weight bringing the alarm clock into view once more, and suddenly remembered the appointment he made the previous night. Lacking the vocabulary to scream anything sensible upon missing the second date of his life, he reverted to the four-letter dictionary. "Shit!" His last word, before scrambling like a gazelle in the eyes of a chasing lioness.

Leo bounced out of bed and landed in the khaki shorts he wore the previous day. He struggled to pull a Nike tee shirt out of his stuffed gym bag and seized his University of South Carolina baseball hat off the weathered surface of the dresser. Through the cottage door, he sprinted for the hotel before his alarm clock displayed 10:58. Up the path, through the bushes, back door, lobby, front door, sidewalk, street, sidewalk, steps, O'Mally's; 10:59 tops. He knew it.

Megan sat perched on a stool at the end of the bar chatting casually with the afternoon bartender who prepared for opening. "What's up?" Leo asked unenthusiastically when he approached Megan breathing hard, but concealing it well.

Megan's expression divulged some turbulent emotion other than delight, when she rolled up her sleeve and dropped the bomb. "What does this say?"

Leo first noticed the Swiss Army logo on her watch, and then the hands, which betrayed his guilt, before mumbling, "Twelve o'clock." His heart sank. "I'm really sorry. I must have hit the hour button when I set the alarm last night."

"You expect me to believe that." She fixed her scowl on him like a mother reprimanding her child.

"Well it's the truth. I can't think of an..."

"No, it's not!" She cut him off without the slightest concern for his excuses. "You know what the truth is pal." Suddenly boisterous laughter replaced her feigned anger and the unknown bartender joined in. "The truth is that I saw you running across the street like you were late for your own funeral and I decided every fun day begins with me setting my watch ahead an hour." Her contagious smile offered Leo a hiding place and his embarrassment subsided easily.

"Does 'bitch' ring a bell?" Leo could not help but laugh along with the conspirators, not because he found humor in the antics, but because he lacked any other option.

"Why I resent that. I've never rung a bell in my entire life. Is your bicycle outside?"

"It's still across the street. It's faster by foot and I wanted to get here before your watch struck three."

"Rule number one on the tour is no sarcasm until I actually know your first name."

"It's Leo."

"Ding. Ding. Let's go, Leo."

Leo Smith took his next important step.

He pedaled with occasional ferocity and steady indifference, touring an island with a woman he hardly knew in a place he barely remembered. His insecurities moved and shifted faster than his bicycle, while the wind played tricks on his thoughts. Feeling the awkwardness of a thirteen-year-old awaiting his first kiss, Leo followed Megan. His expectations fluttered from the traditional, to the X-rated while he watched the figure of a woman attacking and defeating each inch of pavement. The ride might have tired him if he thought of it, but he never did. He simply followed closely and continued to examine the woman who rushed into his life without invitation on the very first day of his voyage.

Leo could not measure Megan, as Dickens would, by comparison only, because the normative group consisted of one high school senior, a five-hour date, and fifteen intense, interrupted minutes. Megan climbed the hills of the Southeast side of the island with effortless ease her thin athletic figure ignoring the urge to sweat in the summer heat. Her sheer, white, cotton blouse ducked under her backpack then fell over loose, olive, shorts as she ascended, and more than anything else, she looked comfortable, not just with her clothes, but with herself. Her lustrous, auburn hair, pulled back tightly with a simple elastic, exposed tan shoulders which befriended the sun. Leo enjoyed this opportunity to observe her without notice while another endless sea of questions flowed through his mind. Without words, he tried to be himself and that most of all seemed dangerous.

"So where are you taking me?"

"The beach."

"I hate the beach." He wished the words had not escaped.

"Not this beach. I made lunch so we can eat by the water and be on our merry way before you have time to hate." In her reply she both answered him and ignored him, in a casual manner that made him grateful.

Once out of town the scenery along the winding road changed dramatically reflecting the island's original beauty, ignoring the tourism controlling Old Harbor. Small bushes, sea grass, and sand bordered the road, instead of sidewalks, day-trippers, and hotels. A soundless ocean excused itself into the background while Leo stretched to hear it and the road turned away. No sounds were audible, but Leo found himself listening anyway. He could not remember these relentless golden hillside scenes from his childhood and that seemed impossible when he thought about nature and creation. The road continued to wind up the hill and the horizon reached past the most capable vision. Leo thought of ships sailing off the end of the world.

"You know I lived on this island until I was almost twelve and I never noticed the quiet out here." The thought escaped his lips unintentionally and represented a new opening previously hidden.

"You're not going to throw some inner peace philosophy at me are you?" Megan also wished she said something else. Understanding the fragile balance of a teetering young man, she would try to hold her sarcasm in check.

Leo dropped, like the land behind him, back into reserved silence. As they rode to the top of the hill, he looked out over the expansive ocean excitedly, knowing he could be looking at Europe or Africa. He enjoyed the idea of an invisible landmass in the great distance, but became depressed feeling it closer than the end of his trek. He once again acknowledged in his precise vision that his father was not the challenge. The Grand, the island, Sarah Parsons,

Megan the bartender, none of them were the challenge. Europe was much further than he thought.

MOHEGAN BLUFFS OVERLOOK
120 Feet Above Sea Level

Leo assumed the sign at the beginning of the path impressed the tourists and particularly their children. The name on the sign identified an island attraction, but the height seemed superfluous to him. He wondered if any sightseers noticed the insignificance of the measurement. Denver plays football a mile up, he thought to himself.

"We're here. Now do you remember this place, Leo?"

"It sounds familiar." An unconvincing response.

"Jesus, Leo, you were almost a teenager when you left here. How could you not remember the bluffs?" She picked on him more than she questioned him. "It's the most scenic spot on the whole island. How do you miss that in eleven years?"

"Scenery doesn't really cut it with the eleven-year-olds. I know it's hard for you to remember back that far, but I was a bit more concerned with jumping off the jetty and the upcoming appearance of hair in strange places." Leo felt satisfied noticing the look of exasperation clouding Megan's confident expression. "You may have told me already but I've forgotten whether Dickinson's poetry or Renaissance art lighted your pre-adolescent torch. Maybe that explains why your sewing those oats now, bartender."

"Okay, okay. So you've never seen the bluffs. You don't have to make fun of me."

"I know I don't have to, but I see how much you enjoy it." Now Leo tested. "So what exactly did you like when you were eleven?"

"I know the amber glow of the fading sun tickled my fancy in the summers of my discontent." She agreed to reserve her sarcasm, not dispatch it all together. Megan locked her bike to the wooden rack and raced down the path before Leo found time to respond. Thankful she sprinted away, knowing he reserved no witty response, he submersed himself in the certainty that something ridiculous would have leaked from his lips.

He caught her by the top of the stairs where he quickly learned *120 feet* translated into a lofty vertical drop. As they sped playfully down the stairs, conversation seemed necessary so Leo began.

"So, where are you from?" The awkward beginning reminded him of dinner with Susan Watts.

"Ah, polite conversation. I wondered when this would begin. I'm from Zephyr Hills, Florida. Where are you from?" She asked the question with the condescending tone of an elderly woman interviewing a toddler. Her voice conveyed insult in Leo's mind but she intended to express the gamesmanship of icebreaking on a first date. Leo, unfamiliar with most tactics of dating, experienced one undeniable emotion. Total, utter frustration.

"Basically, what I would like to know is who the hell you are. You appear out of nowhere." He abruptly saw the future of a man looking back on the past knowing he blew it. The vision failed to stop him. "Why am I here right now? Am in the web of the Block Island spider woman?"

"Nothing that dramatic," she interjected ignoring the tension in his voice. "If I remember correctly, you walked into my bar."

"I'm not quite sure how things work around here, but where I'm from female bartenders don't make lunch dates with seventeen-year-old strangers they know nothing about. How about if I learn something about you that doesn't appear on your driver's license?" Leo could not recollect when or how he became so angry.

Without wrath or surprise, Megan turned around, looked up the steps at Leo, and avoided the temptation to ask how many female bartenders he actually knew. "I hadn't guessed it would be this bad. You really don't know what to think. You've got all the normal insecurities a teenager feels and quite a few more, don't you?"

Don't you? It hung in the air not as a question between new friends, but as a statement of absolute certainty, and Leo noticed the difference. There was something about Megan he needed to learn. "Are you going to continue with your analysis doctor?"

"I'm hungry," she said with the calmness of a woman who knows complete control. "Lunch is being served at the bottom of the stairs."

As he watched Megan descend the stairs, Leo cursed himself for his inability to turn away. He cursed Megan for the delicate power she possessed, and then reluctantly, and willingly, he followed. They might protest, lobby, and complain how men run the world, but in the heart and mind of every woman there lies true understanding of the word power. When they use it, men bend.

"It's good to hear from you, Miss Fortun."

"Well, I wish I had some wonderful news to report but I don't." Sarah Parsons never expected any wonderful fruition of answers from this life experiment with Leo and his father, but she offered thanks for the early update. "Not very much has happened so far I'm afraid."

"Has there been any change at all?"

"I don't believe so, Sarah. Leo hasn't rested since he's been here. He still needs to find his way around a bit. I saw Richard earlier today and the poor fool looked as if he'd been in a fight. That seemed strange even for him."

"Is he all right?"

"Well, he looks fine. I'm sure if he'd been drinking..."

"I'm sorry, Miss Fortun," she cut her off. "I meant Leo."

"Of course, dear. I'm sorry."

"I don't mean to be rude, but he's only seventeen and I worry what this will do to him."

Maude Fortun let out a brief sigh sounding unmistakably like a laugh. "Are you listening to yourself, Sarah? Only seventeen. I don't think anyone needs to hold his hand and if anyone does it certainly isn't you or me."

Sarah joined Maude's laughter with a soft chuckle. "Just look out for him, okay?"

"Leo, can look out for himself." Without knowing why, she expressed herself with complete conviction.

"Do you think so?" Sarah knew she sounded ridiculous, but age could not cushion the blows Leo endured in the last week. She saw her son only as a callow young boy with a lot to sort out.

"I know so, Sarah, and so do you. Now you take care and I promise to keep you posted on that *little boy* of yours."

"Good bye, Miss Fortun." Sarah allowed the phone to drop from her hand, and watched helplessly as it dangled in the air with the support of the cord still in her hand. The weightlessness of the phone intensified the weight on her shoulders, and she wished from the corner of her kitchen that support for her son could be offered just as easily from her arms. She lost focus staring at the wearisome place mats on the table as the walls moved away, and she stood immersed in the center of it all. Alone and afraid for the first time in her life, she replaced the phone on the receiver cutting her only connection to the island.

When Maude Fortun dropped the phone into place, she rethought the disturbing vision of the surreal scene on the street from the previous evening. In the hotel kitchen, and through the windows of the morning's darkness, she pondered how difficult it must be to knock down your own father. Richard Smith, unable to cure his own pain, needed someone to get him feeling again. Even if Leo and Richard denied every bond, they were still inevitably a father and son. Miss Fortun turned and looked out at the cottage. Leo Smith had a future to plan and embrace, a best friend to mourn, and a life to begin; yet he settled for the summer in the small town of New Shoreham to help a man he no longer knew. An aging woman with a strong will felt somewhat proud of the young man, and increasingly thankful to him for a lesson learned so late in life.

Leo's pride forced him to lag a few steps behind Megan. She already placed a blanket across the mild and inviting sand when he reached the beach. He stared down at his feet sinking into the grains of warmth with each step, refusing to accept an errant glance from the woman who won this round. The rocks mixed in the sand existed as targets to hold Leo's focus until a more solid form of God's work interrupted.

"I see you decided to join me for lunch." Her persistence exhausted him.

"I couldn't find a better offer on the way down. A few more stairs and you may have lost me."

"It wouldn't surprise me." *Yes, it would*, he thought.

Both Megan and Leo worked diligently to avoid an apology or any simpler sentiment offering regret. "A hundred-and-forty-four steps and no good offers. I must be losing my touch." The torturous tingles from head to foot held Leo when Megan looked at him as if the crowded beach and the withering bluffs ceased to exist. "I needed something to keep me busy on the way down since I didn't have you annoying me anymore and counting stairs..." He paused, glancing at the horizon to find a new beginning.

"I'm sorry about what I said. You were right about me. I've just got a lot to deal with."

She allowed him the last sentence knowing the importance, but saved him from stumbling again with an understanding interruption. "I hope you're working up an appetite with all that self-revelation." Eyes locked, she continued. "I owe you an apology too, Leo. I haven't exactly told you everything. I know why you're here. The Fortun gals and I have been sharing conversation for a few years now and Margaret explained why you were coming."

Leo observed nothing in the course of the delightful day that prepared him for this revelation when his face dropped and his soul fell open on the beach. In a disheartening sentence he understood her interest, and cursed himself for believing more attractive possibilities. "So you were asked to take on the new island charity case. I appreciate the pity, but I think I can get through this without a social worker." In the midst of his unobservable anger toward her staged sympathy, and his embarrassment for believing in sincere intentions, Leo turned and walked away.

"No, you can't." The tone of her voice remained even and calm but actions revealed her own fiery emotions. She reached into her bag for red, delicious ammunition and fired an apple at Leo. Aim failed to match velocity and the apple screamed past him before exploding against a rock near the edge of the bluff. The struggling teenager never acknowledged the pitch.

"Is that your solution, tough guy? Big, bad, and mad at the world." Children and families who arrived and descended to enjoy the peace of the famed Mohegan Bluffs redirected their attention. "I'm not here for pity you infantile, self-absorbed moron." He stopped, quickly turning back to face Megan and the undeniable truth that she went too far. Her apprehension appeared clearly in her expression when she absorbed the anger, the hate, and the distress in his face. His reaction surpassed anything for which she prepared in her attempt to regain his attention. He was passive.

His words proclaimed the irrefutable fact known only by those with sound experience, not the experience of years or time, but the experience of a singular horror parallel to that New York morning. "You don't know," he said. "There is no way you could know." Leo felt the sand between his toes as a substitute for sentiment and refused the notion to move either toward or away from her.

"That's right." Megan''s voice calmed, in natural and logical agreement with his. "You're right. I don't know. I'm not here to pretend I know. I'm not here because you earned my sympathy when I heard the story of some lost and troubled boy. I'm here because you've earned my respect. You're doing the right things, Leo. I'm sure you loved him very much." She did not know which lines she could cross safely until she expressed herself and surveyed his reaction. With the greatest damage done, she lacked the time to be timid. Leo neither confirmed nor dismissed her worry when his eyes enveloped her as if she disappeared from view and, despite her uneasiness, she continued carefully. "When I was your age, I used to spend summers with my friends smoking pot and sponging off my parents, and something tells me I wasn't the only teenager in the history of the world ignoring the lonely guilt of indifference. Sometime between now and then I've done some growing up, but I'm still not sure I could handle what you're going through. I know you're alone out here, Leo, and I thought maybe you could use a friend, but I honestly have no desire to befriend you if you think I'd be here out of pity. I refuse to stay with someone who respects me so little, no matter how much I admire him. So the choice, like every other one you've made so far, is yours. Lunch? Or a hundred-and-forty-four stairs?" For the first time on that hot, June day, small beads of sweat appeared on Megan's forehead.

In Leo's mind she betrayed him, and lied to him, before finally confessing herself and her lack of understanding. In the last week of his life both catastrophic and commonplace events forced him to mature by the hour, but on this day he would rely on an asset belonging more to children than adults. *Trust*. In a crucial standoff, where he believed he could turn and walk away from this determined and complete woman without ever thinking of her again, he allowed himself three simple words: "What's for lunch?"

"We're down an apple but everything else is delicious." Her statement escaped in the brevity of a strong exhale as she now noticed, in anticipation of his response, she held her breath. "This might even be the beginning of a great friendship."

"Don't try that friendship line on me, Megan. I've heard it a million times."

The two sat in silence, as a rest from the necessary and powerful words that exhausted their third meeting in two days. Leo enjoyed a fictitious thought, believing the Mohegan Bluffs rather than heated conversation left him speechless, and ignoring the truth for a long gaze, he wondered when glaciers became artists. The two friends, regaining comfort, watched the waves break over the rocks while the gulls hunted whatever floated dangerously close to the surface of the sea, or drifted too far from a tourist's blanket. Megan thought about Leo and the respect she never planned to confess. She believed she could help Leo, mostly because it seemed more plausible than believing any one person facing the storm alone.

Leo thought quietly of fathers and sons. It amazed him that worthwhile memories of himself and his father could be accessed through this island. The island and their relationship still represented no more than a flicker of light in a distant past of darkness. With great clarity, Leo understood that fatherhood could not be characterized solely by a relationship, or exclusively by genetics. Somehow the combination of whiffle ball and dominant traits led to celebrating a day in June, and by those standards he knew no father, but he could try to find him. On this excursion he could share days with Richard, but the culmination of even their best times might not make him a father. Slowly, Leo began feeling regret, not because he missed the fantastic traditional relationship, but because he did not. Neither a game of catch, nor a detailed comparison of the family jaw line could unlock the gate to his path, the key was far more important.

"Walter," Leo whispered as the cliffs, the sand, and the ocean surrounded him again

"What did you say?" Megan broke the silence.

Leo recovered. "I said, 'what's this?'" Leo picked up a piece of unfamiliar fried food.

"You've never had it before?"

"No," said Leo.

"Well, try it and find out you big baby. I'm sure you'll love it." Her lips released the words and formed a smile which struck Leo in the depths of the feelings he never knew, and in the surface of his skin, as he felt himself blush without embarrassment.

"I'm not used to trusting people when it comes to the unknown." Clearly, he now tried too hard.

She ignored the awkwardness of his statement and continued. "Then this will be two new experiences for you and hopefully a lot more to come." The words hung in the air and they both accepted the canyon of dissimilarity between the natures of their experience, without sharing their thoughts. Silence conveyed the message better than words and they both thought of new experiences in their future together. Leo dropped the calamari into his mouth without further doubts and enjoyed the rest of his afternoon in the sun.

The two friends stood in front of O'Mally's noticing, but not watching, the three o'clock ferry move out into the harbor. They spent four hours together exchanging lifetimes of information, without sharing the simplest details. Friendship evolved with the swiftest necessity out of unavoidable, indisputable hardship. Sometimes it *is* a day at the beach.

"I'm due into work in a few minutes so I've got to head inside." Megan's nervousness became obvious, standing like an employee waiting for the boss to scold. Any traditional ending to their modern tragedy would have belittled their day with vulgarity, and they knew it well. They could not hug, kiss, or shake hands because healing history often means walking away.

"I guess I'll try and catch a few hours sleep before I start on my second joyous night watch."

"Very enthusiastic. Listen, Leo, I'm going off island for a few days but I hope we can see each other again when I get back."

"I'm not yet needed elsewhere."

"I hope you're able to get some things worked out." She would have rather ended the conversation without the resounding note of a therapist, but she wanted him to hear her mean it. The conversation began to fade so Leo simply turned and walked into the future.

"I hope so too." Megan heard the mumbled statement not intended for her ears, and wished her best thoughts upon her new friend in pain.

Chapter 13
Walden

Leo fell asleep after reading almost a hundred more pages in *The Autobiography of Malcolm X*. Far from restful, his sleep arrived in short intervals, and remained vacant of any dreams. Perhaps a cluttered mind leaves little room for dreaming. When his alarm clock sounded thirty minutes before work, he awoke unprepared for his eight-hour battle against the night. Battles already lost are toughest to fight.

He rose and stumbled across the uninviting room and stared down into a once white sink, now forever tainted with a thick brown ring. He brushed his teeth while thinking how hard it had become to look into a mirror. Rather than continue to expose himself to vulnerability, he turned a mouthful of toothpaste into a mirror-full with one thick *splat*. "What are you doing here? What can you possibly accomplish?" The rhetoric continued to flow from his mouth extending from his acrimonious mind and the foamy mirror-mirror on the wall provided no answers.

The hotel lobby quieted by 1:00 a.m., so Leo found an uncomfortable spot on the weathered front steps to investigate his sanity. There in the front of the hotel he wondered when he would see his father again. Unavoidable, he faced the solemn thought that years passed with less thought of his father than the last two days. He wanted desperately for Richard to find some semblance of order in his life, but he knew one punch solved nothing. With the image of his unconscious father fresh in his mind, he remembered the "long-term plan," but on the steps patience yielded helplessly to contrivance.

Shirking responsibility, and better judgment, Leo locked the door of the hotel and strolled across the street to O'Mally's. Confronting the lion in his own den offered the most direct way to solve a problem. He could not wait for his father to come to him, he needed to be the aggressor. His passive nature betrayed him in many memories and in the street he could see regret as one of the few permanent emotions. Leo knew his father faced plenty of problems without having to seek out his son and offer his pride for pounding. No one ever offers himself as a sacrifice to the volcano, someone has to get him out of the jungle. Leo knew the fight against alcohol would not be easy for Richard so he entered the jungle to confront the lion.

The moonless night concealed the man slumped against the side of the pub, and if not for the wad of spit that splattered upon, and stuck to his cross-trainers, Leo would never have noticed him. He looked down disgusted at the man who just launched a hawker onto his *Adidas* and opted for sympathy before rage, addressing the man politely. "Excuse me, sir, but you really need to watch what you're doing." No response. "Excuse me!"

He felt certain that no productive answer would come from this man, who like his bottle of *Wild Irish Rose*, was half in the bag. The man's two flannel, plaid shirts and dark, blue jeans again seemed incongruous on that warm June evening. His long hair covered most of his face as well as the red bandanna tied around his head.

"Hey, Woodstock child! Are you alive or was that airborne saliva your last tribute."

"It's part of the island hospitality," the answer came. "You give me five bucks and I'll shine them for you."

Leo's maximum tolerance peaked at a dangerously low level on this night and the man supporting the building refused to help his own cause. "How about I return the saliva to it's original home with an unusual amount of speed and force due to its newfound propulsion system. My foot, to be exact."

"Sweetest things turn sourest by their deeds, my boy. You know you're on the right track. Your dad's a good man who needs your help but isn't sure if he deserves it." He paused. "Don't look so confused, kid, it's a small place and people talk. The rest of it I'll put together myself." The man slowly climbed to his feet clinging to the wall as the only means of aiding his balance.

"Sweetest things," Leo recognized the phrase from Shakespeare and began wondering to whom exactly he spoke. The man spit on his shoes, quoted Shakespeare, and offered advice on family matters, all while pounding a bottle of high-octane liquor. "Who are you?"

"If it looks like a duck and walks like a duck it ain't always a duck kid. Defy the clichés. By the way, you might want to try and get settled yourself before you start working on Pop's troubles."

"Do you have a name, Woodstock?"

"Yeah, but I hate it," the man grumbled walking away. He managed about ten paces while Leo continued to consider the man who remained an enigma. Leo's concentration broke when the man yelled back, "Call me Walden," then not quite so loudly, "I bet I'd like that."

Leo dismissed the event in the street as a strange but unimportant occurrence in the greater scheme. His efforts to put the mysterious man out of his mind made the act much harder. Two things remained certain; he would be thinking about Walden, and Walden would be back. He entered O'Mally's.

The crowd moved in waves barely contained by the walls, but the room seemed empty to Leo. The only two people in the world with whom he wished to talk were painfully absent from the melancholy scene. He forced his way through the sea of drunks without giving a thought to the spilled drinks and muffled curses that trailed him. When he finally reached the bar the unfamiliar face behind the mahogany looked less than concerned with his plight. "Who?"

"Richard Smith. He used to be the night watchman across the street at The Grand."

"Oh, that old drunk. Don't think I've seen him tonight, but you can be sure he'll be back."

Leo never jumped at the opportunity to say kind things about his father but he instantly soured with the sound of a stranger insulting Richard. "The drunk is my father, assface, and any verbal assault on him might result in a physical assault on you." Leo had never been in a real fight in his life. The knockout blow to his father represented the first punch he threw since the grade school playground, but something intrinsic reverberated in his voice forcing the bartender to respond.

"He was in here before but he went home." The bartender casually turned and assumed his position as God to the ritual drinkers.

Home. Leo had not considered for one minute of the last forty-eight hours where Richard currently lived. Unable to locate where his father resided on an island consisting of twenty-one square miles seemed a pathetic notion. "How can I possibly help someone I can't even find?" The thought rang in his ears, finding perpetual failure at every step in his journey, and he remained uncertain of his next productive move. After only two days, a young inexperienced boy already concerned himself with ineptitude, while walking out of a drink-tank. Slowly, his thoughts swayed in the late air of the street, as he emerged from the bustling bar. Only two days. Walden's warning echoed in his ears as he moved up the street in torrid strides. *By the way, you might want to try and get settled yourself before you start working' on Pop's troubles.* The flashback served Leo as another rare soothing moment.

With the rising of the sun came the turning of the last few pages of *Malcolm X.* Leo's watch ended with a rattle of pots and pans sounding the early morning movements of overworked old women. After two restless hours of sleep in the cottage, he awoke to chuckles of children with pails and shovels dominating the beach thirty yards away. He spent the morning daydreaming sporadically, while ceaselessly thinking of New York City. He wondered how different his life would appear without the influence of his best friend. Malcolm X was just one example. Having completed the autobiography, he regretted that he probably would have never read the account if not for the nagging of his beautiful, late friend.

Any knowledge Leo previously attained with regard to the life of Malcolm X would have come from the same people who said, "That black kid sure can play basketball. It'll be his ticket to college." He heard that El Hajj Malik El Shabazz supported racism stating white men were the devil. Some would try and convince people that X represented for African-Americans what the Ku Klux Klan represented for Caucasians. "Half the truth is a lie," Leo contemplated aloud. The things that wouldn't have reached his field of vision were the looting of a home, the slaying of a father, a very partial trial, and the racism experienced by a young boy. These were the things that were lost in conversations, hidden in fact "by any means necessary." Leo would read the whole story, perhaps glamorized, but through the eyes of the great man himself. All praise was due to a young man with a developing jumpshot who loved to read. Only the mistakes had been Leo's. He missed his brother.

Leo spent the first part of the afternoon surveying the carefully maintained town that embarrassed the beauty of the surrounding scene. The countless shops and restaurants blended together but Leo knew better than to group things for appraisal. Each store built a personality of its own, some more personable than others. Tourists scurried along the streets hoping for the perfect souvenir no one else grabbed, but they were all previously considered. All the great gifts turned into tee shirts and bumper stickers year after year. Originality ceased to exist in this part of the island and nothing is *re*created well. Leo wandered into a bookstore where he scanned the shelves excited that he read more books than he ever took time to notice. The top three books on the paperback best-seller list were digested more than a year ago. Delving further into the bookstore revealed that it was quite large for a small island. After a brief perusal, Leo found a small laminated card that read "Book, Line, and Sinker Best Buy." Unable to resist the title, Leo picked up *Zen and the Art of Motorcycle Maintenance: An Inquiry into Values.* "Not for me," he laughed to himself, "I don't have any values."

"The extraordinary story of a man's quest for truth." Leo did not seek the truth. He only wanted answers and the validity of those answers was secondary in his struggle. He continued to read, "The fabulous journey of a man in search of himself." Sold.

"Good afternoon," Leo smiled pleasantly as he could at the very attractive woman behind the counter. Her pale skin and long, brown hair contradicted the Block Island climate. She appeared an ideal companion for mythical Icarus as her skin, and the Irish wool sweater she wore, seemed impervious to heat. The pretentious look on her face convinced Leo he dealt with a woman who believed she knew more than she did. This woman undoubtedly emanated the capacity to combine her average beauty and fraudulent intellect to win a good man who consumed too many beers. More than the stunningly beautiful or the truly intellectual, such women are dangerous.

"So you'll be attempting to read 'Zen' will you?"

"Any good?"

"No, it's not *any good*, as you say." Yale graduates across the country could not better her condescending attitude. "It's a voice of a generation. Pirsig explains the seventies in the vernacular of those who lived through those years; people who felt what he felt. I think you're going to need an interpreter, young man."

Anticipating her arrogance, Leo became surprised only by the direct manner in which the woman spoke: her lack of all subtlety. Nevertheless he was armed. "Wow, that's really impressive. I've always wanted to be a person more like you, but I just couldn't work it out."

"Don't worry, kid, being an intellectual isn't all it's cracked up to be." Leo could foster no idea why this woman would attempt to chastise him, but he recognized the patterns of people who hate to look in the mirror. Hers was a self-confidence built in the belittling of others, a bad choice for this cashier.

"Oh no, the intellectual part is easy. I could read a few book jackets, adorn some thick glasses, and regurgitate the creative thoughts of others. Those things alone fool the world. The problem is vertigo. I'm afraid of heights." He kept his quarry guessing.

"And what, may I ask, does that have to do with intellect. I can only assume your speaking metaphorically of ascertaining certain heights." So easily frustrated.

"I wouldn't dare. You see a person like yourself has no problem sitting yourself way up high on that pedestal of yours. Even if that pedestal is in a small bookstore on an obscure Atlantic island, rather than a research laboratory, a museum of fine arts, or a publishing house, you still have no problem propping yourself up. You and your inflated sense of self have absolutely no problem looking down on the townsfolk or peasantry if you will. That's the part I don't think I'll never understand and it's killing me. Here is what I would love for you to explain to this troglodyte." He paused looking down over the counter in the direction of the woman's hips, which were not quite so slim as in her younger years. "When you're way up there with the aristocracy gazing down, how is it that you balance your giant ego and excessive lower body weight on the pedestal without falling over backwards? Maybe if I gave old Pirsig a call he could write an inquiry into that. You, of course, could be my interpreter." Leo dropped a ten-dollar bill on the counter and walked out of the store without looking back. The flabbergasted woman remained completely silent until Leo nearly collapsed halfway up the street, doubled over, laughing loudly. In a strange way, he felt like a child again.

He spent the rest of the afternoon on the breakwall thinking, reading, and just staring blankly into the day. Unlike other congested hours he read vociferously with great concentration. His night at The Grand came and went quietly like passive tides, only intensifying the loneliness. The uneventful hours of another day passing reminded him that he continued to move, backwards.

Chapter 14
Hoops

Leo wrapped a towel around his waist and trudged along the hallway to the bathroom. As was the case with just about everything in Leo's abode, these facilities were moderate, bordering on unacceptable. The lone window painted shut long ago lacked curtains, blinds, or anything at all to keep the outside world from looking in. The grout in the tiled floor yielded an obvious crawl space for many members of the insect world. Disinfectant scattered throughout the room cleaned nothing, serving only as a signature from one of the fraudulently thorough chambermaids who knew neither Maude nor Margaret Fortun would spend a single minute in the cottage all summer. The disinfectant cut the smell of mildew enough to emulate the aroma of a fur tree, in a garbage can. The look and smell of the room would have enraged any guest of the hotel. Leo never noticed. With a long, arduous, obstacle-riddled road still ahead on this journey, where he hung his hat or washed it, no longer mattered to Leo Smith.

Out of the shower and back in his room, Leo stepped into the same pair of shorts he wore every day since his arrival and a plain, white, Gap tee shirt that actually smelled clean. He glanced in the mirror without breaking either of the two strides it took him to cross the room. He donned *The Gamecocks* hat, now a permanent fixture on his head, and started off toward the hotel.

In a few short days, Leo became so accustomed to the rhythm of the ocean through the cover of tall bushes, he could determine the tide without vision. Through anything, he knew the sound of the small waves would always comfort him. The fact seemed incontrovertible as his strides strengthened, life could be worse than spending an unsupervised summer by the ocean. The experience would complete Leo's adolescent life and the summer would force the inevitable. Becoming a man. Entering through the back door of the hotel, Leo saw the familiar sight of Margaret Fortun sitting comfortably in her eternity at the large kitchen table.

"Good morning."

"Good morning, Leo," she replied turning toward him. She should have been startled by the unannounced entrance, but never flinched, relaxing safely in the space around her. The kitchen more than the hotel itself belonged to her or, perhaps she belonged to it.

"I suppose I can be fairly certain you haven't eaten yet. There are some cold cuts in the refrigerator to make a sandwich." They were only words, but they made the sound of a blanket tucking a child in on a cold night.

"Thank you." Leo moved across the room toward lunch. "Miss Fortun, could you please tell me where my father lives?"

"Oh, Leo, he's lived here year round for quite some time now. I don't know if he even keeps a place anymore."

"Actually, I wanted to know where he lives on the island, not the mainland."

She looked at Leo like an inquisitive boy asking why the sky is blue. He could not have understood her expression or her movements until he heard the answer to his question "Leo, your father lives right above you out in the cottage. You must have known that. Two people living that close have to run into each other eventually, even in this short of a time."

He uttered the sentence aloud, without speaking to Miss Fortun. "Not if one of those people is trying to avoid the other." A distinct feeling exists in the world, exposed only when a person understands they are being avoided. Leo now experienced that feeling, as most people have, but the sting penetrated deeper into his heart with the realization that his own father avoided him. He would eat quickly.

Now he walked with more than a spring in his step back down the path to the cottage. Exhausted questions raced through his mind and anything seemed possible if his careless father could avoid him so easily. His aggravation, directed mostly at himself for never noticing the obvious, forced his temper to rise like mercury in a thermometer gravitating toward the sun. He climbed the aging, back stairs of the building ascending toward his father's room, knocking on the door twice before the sickly voice replied, "Who is it?"

"The Black Plague. Don't worry though, Leo's not here so it's safe to let me in."

As the bolt clicked on the opposite side, Leo pushed open the door and flooded into the room. Once past his father, the process of understanding began. An empty bottle of Jack Daniel's whiskey rested awkwardly on the floor near Richard's meticulously made bed. Similar contradictions filled the entire room. Slightly larger than Leo's domicile, the lack of space was coupled with detailed character. The two bookshelves on the wall overflowed with volumes but not a single book looked out of place. The hard and soft cover bindings opened and closed many times evidenced by the faded titles and authors. Two Eshcer prints sandwiched a framed Monet over the bed. An empty case of Piel's bar bottles cowered in the corner at the foot of the mahogany dresser. Jim Beam rested comfortably, the closest companion of the plants flourishing on the windowsill. The room, both light and dark, boasted walls splashed with color to befriend the black and white tiles of the small kitchen area and the polished wooden floor. The small one room apartment, his father's home, demonstrated a living, breathing contradiction. Leo did not check his premises.

Richard Smith, seemingly ashamed of his exposed life, did not speak to his son when he entered the room. Looking around, scanning details carefully, Leo stared at a man's problem. He did not hear the grumbling of a child, or see the incompetence of a fool unable to take care of himself. Instantly, the communication gap between two individuals closed, bridged with a son's observation of his father's room. Leo lost sight of a time when the man who lived in that room existed as his father in the most complete sense of the word. He caught a brief glimpse of that loss when he satisfied himself sufficiently that this was not the home of a bum. In the short time since crashing through the secret door, Leo noticed carpeting, painting, picture frames, and a bookshelf where he previously accepted the ineptitude of a job done poorly. The change in attitude grew in his words. "You don't have to avoid me, Richard, I'm not the enemy."

He allowed his father an opportunity to deal with the fact that his son traveled here to help. The devastated man would have to charge through the shame of his errors and strain to see the determined efforts of his son. And he did. "It's hard for me. You have to understand that I know I never made it as a father, but now I'm failing again. I'm failing myself and I can't stop it."

It took less than a few seconds for Leo to find the proper words. "You passed on your chance to be a father and I'll probably never forgive you for that." He inhaled deeply. "I don't think I can. Taking a swing at you the other night felt good. It felt real good, but it's the last thing I want. I've managed to struggle past the emptiness in my life without your help so far and I'm sure I'll make it the rest of the way, but it's not our only choice. Anyway, I'm not sure our relationship is really the issue right now."

"So what is the issue?"

Leo's mind thrashed at hundreds of answers but he grew weary of his own sagacious words. He could only offer possibility, not the omniscient answers they both craved. Finally, for his own relief and his father's humility, he decided. "Lunch."

Both men felt a blanket of relief but they knew more trouble awaited them with each step, regardless of intentions. The issues concerning them as a father and son would never reach complete resolution, and ultimately that probably offered the best answer. Without the pressure of fictional happy endings, there would be more time for Leo and Richard Smith to pursue a friendship. Of course, barriers presented themselves on that path as well.

As they walked out of the cottage, Leo decided to avoid any attempts at a serious conversation. "I wish the bushes were still cut back so you could see the ocean from the cottage."

"The problem with that is the eye sore that you and I call home would be visible from the beach. Can't have the hired help within full view of the precious patrons. Perception is everything."

"And how would you perceive us."

"Hungry?"

"Good answer." They could always hide from themselves a bit longer.

Lunch at the *Harbor View* restaurant passed more smoothly than either of them expected in their first real attempt at redemption. Leo and Richard enjoyed each other's company faltering only when Richard ordered a gin and tonic with lunch. A sideways glance from Leo's determined eyes prompted the necessary change and Richard ordered a Coke without another word. A token gesture, but another beginning in a son's search for a man, who might one day become his father. Their conversation shifted from island scenery, to books, sports, and Leo's future, but they spoke without any mention of reconciliation. Richard's final two words before paying the bill were the most important. After five years of limited communication he uttered the simplest and most meaningful phrase of their lives together. "Thank you." While the young man appreciated the gratitude, the words said much more.

After lunch the two men separated, agreeing that Richard would once again work the night watch for The Grand Hotel. Hesitant at first, Leo realized if he refused to trust his father, no one could. He promised himself he would wander through the hotel later to ensure his father's sobriety and physical presence. While willing, he still balked at the idea that three days equaled sufficient time for recovery, but knew all change began with a risk.

Leo meandered up the street, away from Richard, visiting the cottage briefly to procure his new novel, and then drifted toward the harbor. The serenity of the outstretched rocks quickly became his temple of solitude and contemplation. Today his solitude was soon interrupted by the infinitely exasperating presence of a man he did not know. From an undetected hiding spot his voice divulged his secrecy.

"Hey there, Smith." Walden lounged in the high grass surrounding the often-traveled path leading to the break wall. "Have you found yourself yet?"

"Have I been looking?" Leo answered confidently prepared for Walden's verbal bag of tricks.

"I hope so."

"You know, Walden, I don't know who you are or why you've taken this interest in my life. Quite honestly, I'm not certain that I care, but what I would like to know is how a guy who probably spends most of his time talking to an omnipotent bottle in a brown bag knows so much about me."

"Like I said, kid, it's a small island. And you, my friend, should care what I have to say because you will be tested later. Granted, many of the tales I spin or deranged observations I make are the ramblings of a poor player, but if you listen closely you will find your truth. I understand what you see before you on the glassy surface is the down and out personification of all the struggles of mankind. Believe me I understand, but I also know that you, unlike most people, see past the exterior." He took a long deliberate quaff from the open bottle in his wrinkled hand.

"Maybe I do, and maybe I don't, but why does that matter? Why do you care what I think of you? You don't even know who I am." Leo's voice revealed a tentative transformation from curiosity to frustration.

"That's where you're wrong, kid. I do know about you. I probably know more than anyone on The Block. You didn't listen to me the other day. I told you to settle yourself before you try to help anyone else. Listen, what's the one thought repeating itself in your mind over and over again? When you're feeling despair, and you're feeling cheated, who are you thinking about? It's not your father, Leo. Who then? You're a troubled soul, Leo, and if you seek answers to staggering problems, the first place you should look isn't Block Island or The Grand. Then, and only then, the answers will present themselves. If you still can't figure it out, you're the dumbest smart kid I know." Walden shifted his weight and rose to his feet without exerting one muscle in his entire body.

"Who the hell are you?"

He stretched his arms above his head in a single, agile move and feigned exhaustion with his body, while his eyes exuded a picture of complete alacrity. "Nobody. It's the single greatest accomplishment of my entire life."

"Do you ever tell anyone? Will you ever tell me who you are?"

"I do. I will." Walden fell backward into the grass, rolling to his side, offering no attempt to return to his feet or reengage. Leo ignored the tumble and did not speak to him again. He simply turned and faced the ocean with one thought in his mind. The thought formed the answer to Walden's question. *Where was his despair*? Within himself. The irreplaceable part of his life he tried to conceal from his mind lived in his heart. Ultimately, his despair would proliferate from a small unfamiliar alley in a big city. When he could walk out of that alley and live again in prelapsaryian safety, the journey would end, and begin again.

Leo skipped over words and sentences, as his thoughts wandered, while sitting on the rocks by the ocean holding the novel before his eyes. He reached the end of every page only to realize that he did not absorb any of the author's vague intentions. After scanning each page several times, he would go on to the next, never allowing his thoughts to leave his brother. An hour passed and Leo completed six pages, understanding nothing.

"Harboring your thoughts?" Only her voice could have pulled him away from Walter and the confusion he read. Leo spun with exuberant euphoria to see Megan standing in front of him. "That's what I always call it. Whenever I just want to relax and think I come out and sit by the harbor." He got to his feet before he managed a single word and slowly reached around Megan stretching for a point far off in the hazy distance. The embrace could have crushed the will of a tiger, the softest touch Megan ever felt, instantly became the most intimate gesture of a young man's life.

"Don't worry, I have this effect on lots of men." The way she expressed herself provided Leo with new knowledge. Even though she could not possibly conceive any idea of what happened on that wall, Leo believed she understood. In that moment Leo's life continued, not as a perpetual quest for answers, but as an embrace on a pile of rocks extending out into the ocean from a small town in Rhode Island. That made it a good life.

"I miss him so much," were his docile words.

On the beach below the bluffs, she proclaimed to know the whole story about Leo's trek to the island. That declaration proved false as the pain reached deepest in the details. She knew about Walter and Richard, death and drinking, but no one actually knew the whole story, a story Leo needed to tell.

They walked alone along the crowded beach and for the first time he shared the whole story of brotherhood. Megan listened, comforted, and even cried, while the longest hour of the toughest day started all over again. Each word of the conversation meant another dagger in his body, another question mark in his mind, and another hole in his heart. The words were everything he needed.

"It's bad enough that I can't face all my doubts alone, but now I'm using my father as a diversion."

"Leo, you can't keep blaming yourself for everything that's happening in your life. Don't you understand that most people would be too immersed in their self-pity and remorse to even begin facing their problems. Instead you're taking on someone else's as well. There's a fine line between denial and recovery, and I think you know that you're on the healing side of the line. Walter knows, Leo; he knows. You just have to figure out how to settle all this with yourself."

"You're the second person who's said that to me." Leo perceived that following the advice of two strangers needed to start someplace other than his negative thoughts, the place he lived since the police station. To trust the woman who offered friendship and the man who spit on his sneakers, Leo would have to first trust himself.

"Well, I'm sure whoever else gave you that advice is also a very smart person." Megan smiled at Leo hoping he would return the gesture. He did and on this walk the pain subsided.

"Do you play basketball?"

"No, why?'

"That's too bad. If you did, I'd probably be in love." They felt the beginning, not of someone's salvation, or healing, but of a relationship between two people who would grow together from something negative, and become something much the opposite. As she held his gaze, all the problems he needed to confront disappeared for an instant, and he reveled in the beauty before him rather than the ugliness behind. In his youth, he failed to grasp that many problems can be solved meticulously through the concerned eyes of a beautiful woman.

When they returned to town, the sun hovered three hours from the horizon reminding Megan she was fifteen minutes late for work, but she could not rush. When they separated, Leo concentrated completely on the one thing in the world he desired more than anything else. He raced to the cottage, changed into his sneakers and sped away on his bicycle toward the basketball courts.

The Block Island School, which would soon serve Leo as a haven for relaxation, stood on the peak of Briar Hill.

A surprisingly modern facility, at least it would have been if the year was 1940, the school graduated nine students in the previous academic year. Once serving as the Protestant church, now a school, and finally a historical landmark, modernizing the school remained inconceivable to the islanders. Set upon the highest point of the island, the ocean remained visible from every window of the building. Any teacher's nightmare. Leo noticed nothing about the school except two backboards, two rims, and enough people to run full court.

Most of the players on and around the court appeared older then Leo, but like most runs, on most courts, skill would not be measured by age. There were ten people on the court when Leo arrived and nine others waiting on the sideline. Five of them were waiting for the next game and four for the one after. The group consisted mostly of college kids working odd jobs on the island for the summer, and clawing at the chance to continue living away from home. Most players were not much bigger than Leo but the age difference was noticeable anyway. After some hesitation, the final four agreed to let Leo play.

Two games passed deliberately before Leo stepped on the court and prepared for the team that won each of the two previous games. Typical rules of any decent pick-up game dictate that the winning team retains the court and the losers sit. "All right, match up," said one of the players on the other team. "Yeah, we're feeling kind of generous so you guys can have the ball first," said another. Leo simply smiled, having seen everyone play, and knowing he could control the game if he chose.

On the first few possessions of the game, Leo's teammates avoided passing him the ball, but it did not concern him. He just grew more intense remembering the days when Walter and he used to play with the older kids on the playground. This court maintained rules like any other, and a golden one involved earning the right of the ball. Finally, the ball came to Leo. "Here you go, right back to me," one of the other players called, but Leo had no intentions of relinquishing the most prized possession on the court. "All right, junior, let's see what you can't do." Intimidation and trash-talking provided nine-tenths of the law in playground basketball. Leo moved left toward the baseline, cutting back with a deft crossover dribble, before exploding up the middle of the defense. When he kissed the ball off the metal backboard, three defenders stood helplessly in the lane while four teammates mentally resolved their inhibitions about giving up the ball.

"I think all we've proven is what you can't do." Only one player on the court refused the invitation to laugh because he preoccupied himself with wiping the egg off his face.

Once again, now becoming a habit, Leo earned the respect of people he hardly knew and more importantly, as the games wore on, he began to make friends. When darkness finally halted play, Leo spoke briefly with a few of the guys and made convincing, empty promises to see them out at the bars later that night. The most important breakthrough for Leo came from finding a place to be comfortable, where the world ceased to revolve, time stopped, and mental toughness felt easy. Basketball was religion. Leo had found his church.

He ate dinner in the hotel by himself, reading while he waited for his father in the lobby surrounded by history. Leo hardly expected an appearance from dear old dad, and found himself shocked when his father walked through the door at 9:45. Bloodhounds down wind could not sniff a hint of Jim Beam.

"Son, if I didn't know better, I'd say you look a little surprised to see me." Richard relished his brief moment of self-worth and the dim light of the Victorian lobby seemed brighter through the eyes of an impressed young man. The lobby felt more like a home for these two desperate men than they ever expected, because they stood together, and between those walls, ignoring a lifetime of solitude, they could pretend they were family. The cognition that intense progress with alcohol sits on a shelf with other works of fiction escaped Leo. He would never see it coming.

"I wouldn't say I'm surprised, just very pleased. Quite a difference from the other night when we bumped into each other." He reevaluated his father. *Things are getting better*, he thought to himself. Things were actually getting worse.

"Well, I guess you don't need me around here. Rumor has it you've done this job before." The humor and meaning were lost and they both understood that Leo said, "I'm glad you're back on your feet and I was happy to help." For the first time in a long time, Leo felt a sense of satisfaction in believing that maybe tomorrow the world would not end.

Chapter 15
Bluffs

Dear Sarah,

Things could definitely be worse. I think that Richard is really starting to get better. I've only been here a few days and already he's back on the night watch. We had some problems the first few days, but it seems like he's starting to look at life as more than the next bimbo, wearing a bottle of perfume, who walks past on a hot day. I feel like the two of us are connecting better than I expected. It's strange to feel a father. I met a girl but don't worry, I'm scared of her. Stop thinking the worst. I know how you love to make things up. I'll be home before you know I'm gone.

Ducking the apocalypse.
Your loving son, Leo

The postcard of Old Harbor, penned from a bed in a small room in the town of New Shoreham entered a mail box that afternoon, and traveled, intent on becoming a cool pillow, with a mission of resting a mother's weary head. Mission accomplished. Sarah Parsons relaxed completely in the thirty seconds it took her to read it twice, and then she continued to worry about her only son.

The next few days within the sanity of The Grand Hotel passed with a fortunate simplicity allowing for healing. Leo spent every possible minute with the woman who offered to listen to the whole story. Beaches, sunsets, bicycle rides, and strong talks brought fond memories and chased away some unfriendly ghosts. On the nights Megan worked, Leo spent his time reading and thinking about those memories he stirred up. And the ghosts. This necessary time served as the motor to propel his life, powered by the strength of his certitude. He only needed a push or two to get going. New life always does.

Three days after Leo mailed his letter, Sarah Parsons placed an important phone call to The Grand.

"Grand Hotel."

"Hello. Miss Fortun?"

"No." On the fourth ring the chambermaid answered the phone to stop the banging in her head created in partnership by the phone and the liquor from the previous night. "Hang on a second while I see if she's in." In the middle of the day, the Fortun sisters were always in. Unless they visited a church dinner or vacated a fire in the hotel, they spent every day and night with their love.

"Hello. This is Miss Fortun." Maude answered.

"Hello, dear. It's Sarah Parsons."

"Oh, Sarah, how are you? I certainly wasn't expecting to hear from you today. I hope there's nothing wrong. I'd hate to hear something was wrong."

"Oh no. Nothing's wrong at all. On the contrary I think things might be going better than the four of us hoped. I received a letter from Leo a few days ago and he sounds as if he's feeling better. He hasn't been a problem for you at all, has he? Richard said you wouldn't mind, but I'd rather hear it from you."

"He's a wonderful boy, Sarah. It's like a breath of fresh air having a young face around here. Other than mine that is. You know I never believed in this idea the two of you cooked up but I really believe the boy is doing well. I do believe that young man is healing."

The decision to lie to Leo surfaced as the most difficult of Sarah Parsons' life. She knew all along that her son's heart pumped strength enough to take on the fictional problems of Richard Smith, and ultimately, she believed a chance to help facilitated a chance to heal. Throughout their years apart Sarah communicated with Richard regularly about the progress of their child, though Leo never knew it. When speaking of his greatest heartbreak, they considered many paths before opting for diversion, a fresh start, and a new place. It just never felt like the right thing to do. The path of the righteous is often hard to find, but it's never hidden so well as when you lie to your own child. A mother's guilty conscience caved for a son she loved knowing that in places where there are crossroads, there are thin lines.

"I never really knew Leo before, but it seems that boy has become a man. He's ready to take care of himself and his father too. He's welcome here forever, but he's almost ready to come back." Old women know most of the secrets of life, even when they are tucked away in the depths of young minds, but they don't know everything.

"Thank you again. I'll never forget what you've done."

"It may be the most honest thing you've ever said, but people tend to forget lots of things. Be very proud, Sarah."

"I am."

The conversation ended with brief pleasantries. The unknowing topic of conversation released energy and tension on the black top of the Block Island School. As always, Leo possessed the answers to his baffling life in his own mind and in his own hands. Richard and Sarah knew their son had the answers, but believed a diversion would be helpful. Their son knew the same thing. Running up and down the court did not help him forget his loss; it helped him remember.

Journeys are steps. Sometimes they are steps backwards caused by the decisions of the people you love the most. From there, the truth can be learned and the people who show it to you can be celebrated. For Leo, the tour guide through truth would be a gifted one. He would be a strange sort of fellow without a history or a future. He would be found nowhere near those courts. He was nowhere in sight. He was nobody.

The sun stretched for the end of the world and the sky belonged to a color more honest than postcards. The one person, who could have made the scene more beautiful as Leo pedaled down the hill, was the one person who did. Her familiar face and unmistakable walk aided him in noticing her approach. Curves better than the ones at the end of the ocean were only a partial print and Leo enjoyed the whole scene. Megan moved in the foreground of the rapidly darkening sky, though she should have been behind a bar. He knew her schedule already.

"Were you harassing perfectly legal customers about their identification again? I think it might be time to see a professional about this habit you're forming." Leo's heart pumped a beat faster on the street than during any part of the six rigorous games he played. The feeling in his chest proved commonplace each time she approached and he hoped this strange event would never cease.

"Very funny. I come all the way up here to try and find you and all I get are the typical tough guy antics." The humor had become ritual. "Maybe I should just turn around and go back to work. At least at the bar people pay to pick on me." Leo's heart settled and he became more comfortable as they stood closer on the hillside. "We knew things would be slow tonight so they gave the good bartender a night off. They kneel at my feet around that place and they know when the talent needs rest."

"Draw straws?"

"Flipped a coin."

"Using the double headed one again?" They began laughing in a manner belonging to time rather than the spoken words. The combination of chemistry, language, biology and even the brief history schooled them into tranquillity. Walden would have called them soul mates, but never in mixed company. He always feared his meaning would be confused with the romance novel definition where any two people who engage in intercourse in a moving train or a translucent lake are soul mates. Walden investigated souls. After seven unprecedented days, only seven, clearly their relationship evolved beyond his pain and their friendship. Nothing physical ever occurred. It grew from their souls.

"Did you have an agenda, madame, or were you just looking to share your great news about getting out of work."

"I need an interpreter to pry a direct thought from you, but I think what you asked me is whether I plan to spend the night with you or doing something fun. Fortunately, my dance card is empty and I hate fun." They continued to derive joy from the games they played in the wake of confusing situations and practical concerns over a now unavoidable event. There was no doubting, only waiting.

"Why don't you go take the shower you desperately need, and I'll come find you in an hour?"

"Best offer I've had all night." Leo knew nothing of love and failed to recognize a familiar pattern of beginning. Everything happened swiftly on this island, and two young people were crashing together like currents at the north point of the island. However, beginning and fruition live far from one another even when the people remain close. "Are you going back into town?"

"No, I live right up the road." Megan started up the hill and Leo forced himself to deal with the possibility that his favorite bartender did not come to find him at all. The incomprehensible games of a beautiful woman are wonderful games, but also, the most perilous in a young man's life. Megan continued to walk away from the cloud of dust and trepidation engulfing the sweating young man and his bicycle. He simply tipped his baseball cap in the direction of her stride, before he turned and rode down the hill.

Leo moved through the backyard of the hotel in swift, smooth strides, pushing the Trek mountain bike gently, alive with the idea of time spent with Megan. He briefly glanced through the screen in the window fascinated by the light touching the gray streaks of Margaret Fortun's hair. His conversation with Megan heightened his senses and he realized the haunting sight of Miss Fortun belonged in a vault with other treasures. The old woman sat motionless in the dining room with Ann the receptionist, who Leo remembered seeing only twice in seven days. Ann earned no other identity. She answered the phone at The Grand from a small, hidden office and smelled of sun tan lotion. Like the lights on the ceilings, she remained a fixture, and without her, the hotel was in the dark. A valued part of the hotel, sadly in an immovable way, she was nothing else.

"Sarah Parsons called me today." Miss Fortun spoke to Ann but the words stopped Leo abruptly. The brief glance became a deafening leer, and no barricade presented itself, enabling the inevitable eavesdrop.

"Who?"

"Oh dear, Ann. You know exactly who I'm talking about. Leo's mother. Anyway she said Leo sent her a letter saying everything was going great." *Small Island,* Leo thought to himself. With the news came a sense of satisfaction knowing his mother's critical worries could rest. The next words set off new alarms, not for the serene woman across the ocean, but in the curious lad, leaning against handlebars at the window. "She said he doesn't suspect a thing."

"Well, he is still a child. Would you expect something like this if you were a teenager. Parents are supposed to say 'I love you,' not 'I'm an alcoholic. You need to help me.' The whole idea seemed strange to me since the day you mentioned it." In that instant, with no knowledge of her accomplishment, Ann created an identity for herself. Someday she could choose from tiles like *Ann, the Bearer of Bad News,* or *Ann the Destroyer of Hope,* or even *Ann, Who Sucks*, but in that moment she did not choose. She sipped her coffee and knew nothing, reverting back into her own identity.

The two women exchanged no more pleasantries regarding the hoodwinked Leo Smith, now walking between his rampant rage and humiliation, stumbling toward the cottage. His steps were heavy, matching his heart.

Arriving in his room, the inevitable tantrums began. No wall left unpunched, no four letter words unsaid, he accepted the temptation to rant and rave like a spoiled child who did not receive the twentieth Christmas present he really wanted. Leo felt the solitude of an outsider again; the April Fool's Day joke planned by the troop of others who owned him in the deception. The pawn in the conspiracy gasped, and he was unable to handle his wrath in this tragedy. Waves did not break, gulls did not cry, the sand disappeared, and the clean, dry air became a vacuum seizing his breaths from him. They played a game with his tortured existence; motives mattered little, as he convinced himself that everyone involved failed him, while he exerted every muscle, idea, and emotion to help.

More than an hour passed while Leo contemplated the misery of living friendless in the world. A small island became huge and the silence of his nightmare ended with the sound of an alarm clock in the form of a knock at the door. Pain shot through Leo's bones with the realization that *she* was in on the laugh. He forced himself to open the door and receive the traitor who inspired his deepest pangs of emotion.

"How's it going?" were his unemotional words when he opened the door.

"What? No rude comments, no innuendoes. I'm at least fifteen minutes late and all the golden boy can muster is 'How's it going?' I'm unimpressed."

The prerequisite smile never appeared on Leo's face knowing he could not avoid the only issue he wished to discuss. Postponing the inescapable confrontation with Megan would only fuel an already raging, four-alarm blaze. "How did they get you in on it?"

Megan flinched before regaining her composure quickly, and began immediately with a painful explanation. Her words invaded the room with unquestionable clarity and Leo believed the explanations, mostly because he wanted so desperately for her to be true. Her part in the plan was small. Her part in the journey prevailed huge and remained secure for now. "Leo, you have to believe that your parents were only trying to help you." The look on his face expressed the towering evidence that he heard that line before. "I know it's a terrible cliché, Leo, but look at yourself. The confused boy who walked up Main Street seven days ago was a frail shadow of the man standing before me now. Leo, I'll understand if you can't trust me right now, but trust you. Trust what you feel. You're winning. It's the toughest battle of your life and you're winning."

"Why are you here?" The four simple words demanded an explanation of her intentions.

She acquiesced quickly knowing his pent anger subsided momentarily. "I'm not here for your parents. And I'm not here for the Fortun's. You already know that."

"So what now?"

"Dorie's Cove," said Megan.

"What?"

As they walked across the parking lot, Megan described the small beach on the Southwest side of the island known as Dorie's Cove. She stopped casually next to the driver's side door of a white, convertible BMW 325i and Leo made no effort to conceal his surprise. "So this is what you drag around town in. It must be nice." Megan found Leo's words refreshing as his humor signaled the beginning of forgiveness.

"Actually, you know full well that I drag around town, as you call it, on a bicycle. Tonight, however, seemed like a nice night for a drive. Do you object to riding in my car?"

"Not at all. I simply wasn't aware that bartending was such a lucrative business." Daily, Leo either ignored or honestly forgot their age difference, but he could not avoid the realization when Megan issued an unintentional reminder.

"No, Leo, bartending is not a very lucrative business. Neither is teaching, but when you work all year sometimes you're allowed to spoil yourself."

"You're a teacher?" Leo again made no attempt to hide the disbelief he experienced.

"I teach first grade. The door's unlocked." Megan slid in under the ragtop while Leo stood motionless completing the math. *At least twenty-two*, he thought to himself before finally joining Megan in the car.

The five-mile ride to the cove included occasional conversation covering various topics like two artists splattering paint across a once-blank canvas. Neither fecund, nor banal, their chatter entertained them in a soothing natural progression of discourse, query, and as always, laughter. Like most people, Leo felt comforted by the simple fact that someone rode with him who would listen. To him, a booming, indulgent conversation or nail-biting lack thereof, failed to matter when accompanied by the revelation that someone waited to listen. *Megan* waited to listen.

When they stepped onto the undulating, cool sand Leo began to search. "So what do I do now?" Leo asked as he walked with Megan toward the invisible waves, discernible only by the unmistakable sound of the water reaching the land. "Everyone here has been involved in the plan, and I certainly have no place to go on the mainland because Sarah may have started this whole thing." He engaged Megan with an inescapable stare asking for instant gratification. "I'm just not sure of my next move."

"Don't you think that's been the problem all along? I mean isn't that what your parents had in mind. If you weren't here now you'd be in Ledyard deciding your next move." Leo, seeking support more than advice, found himself troubled by Megan's reminder of these *better days*. "After all, if you hadn't come, you would have missed the ever-so-enchanting experience of meeting me."

Megan's valiant effort at reliability turned Leo's bewilderment to disgust. "So you think they were right to trick me into thinking my father battled alcoholism and I was the answer to his problems. It was a good idea to manipulate a non-existent relationship by putting the weight of my own well-being on top of it. The fact still remains that if my best friend in the whole world hadn't died, my father wouldn't give a shit about his poor, estranged son. And honestly, that would have been just fine with me." Leo paused, settling himself, as the expression on Megan's face reminded him of his escalating tone. His feelings had little to do with her, but his broken will rather than his mind controlled his passion. "Do you want to hear my immature seventeen-year-old answer to this whole slice of chaos? Do you want to know what I think?"

"Yes. It's the only thing that matters right now."

"It sucks." Leo finally permitted himself the innocence of not searching for answers. For the first time since the beginning of his road trip, the prospects of resolution and miracles vacated his struggling mind. He completely surrendered in the same manner every human being must at some point relinquish the fight, and take another breath. Unlike any other move he attempted in the past week, it was absolutely necessary.

He turned from Megan and walked back toward the road without reason and without another word. Not knowing how much Leo just accomplished with ultimate brevity, Megan held her stance, content to let him go. In her entire, short adult life, she never doubted her own strength of will, but on that beach her knees became weak and those first doubts crept slowly into her mind. She opened her mouth to scream but failed to make a sound. She dropped the blanket she carried from the car and three steps later experienced the rush of her body in a full sprint.

He never heard her coming. When she tackled him, her momentum forced them to the ground and sand flew in multiple directions through the air. Leo fell sideways and rolled to his back barely noticing the weight of Megan on top of him.

"What the hell are you doing?" The words came immediately and carelessly from the base of his spine sounding most like indifference. His tone failed his sentiments, and the expression of amusement controlling his face became an ultimate gesture of friendship, encouraging her stillness as she relaxed on his chest.

"Don't know." The only speech she could prepare in the fifteen strides it took her to reach him. The succinct movement from her torso to the nape of her neck followed her words downward toward the apprehensive face of Leo Smith. Her kiss followed her declaration filled with all the commotion their friendship created. The jolt that pierced Leo's body, completely foreign to his senses, excused all the mistakes a lifetime could manufacture. Nothing like the experienced Susan Watts, Leo felt the kiss, and the embrace, of a woman. One simple, short kiss remains an ultimate, uncorrupted experience of youth in which friendship and doubt are replaced by an indescribable feeling that fades slightly with each kiss there afterwards. Love, marriage, fidelity, and certainty have no place in the first exchange and the experience of beginning is like no other.

No problems or journeys crowded the beach that night. No sex or declarations of love clouded the immense splendor of the starlit sky. The waves failed to crash into time and separate these two friends from the rest of the world. Megan and Leo never discussed dreams and visions on the beach that night. They spoke briefly about the color of bicycles and great dinners. The world never stopped on the beach that night. It continued to turn on its axis, as embarrassing childhood stories, and boring days were discussed. In the course of time, they experienced one another on a beach like any other beach, on a night like any other night. Only their relationship was special. Megan told wonderful stories and Leo Smith relaxed completely for the first time in a week.

A few rays of sunlight broke through the cloud cover waking Leo from a long three-hour stretch of sleep. He felt the exaltation of a child finding eggs on Easter seeing Megan on the blanket next to him, understanding that it was no dream. Without another thought, he leaned over and kissed her softly on the cheek. In the next forty minutes, he divided his time staring back and forth at this divine woman and the sinking horizon before him.

"What did I do to deserve the kiss?" Staring out at the ocean, Leo did not notice Megan sitting up behind him.

"She lives. I wasn't sure you'd ever wake up."

"Hoping to really take advantage of me," she smiled.

"Very funny," said Leo nervously. "Do you have to work this morning?"

"Yeah, Smith, the bar opens at 7:00. Stop avoiding my question. What did I do to deserve it?"

"I just wanted to say 'thank you.' I really enjoyed last night. I know it sounds stupid, but I'm not used to talking like that. I really think it...Well anyway, thanks."

She enjoyed his awkward explanation more because of his awkwardness than his explanation. "Where I'm from people normally wait until I'm awake to say thank you."

Unlike the conversations from the previous night, Leo wanted this one over as quickly as possible. "Sorry."

"Oh, no no. Too easy, Mr. Smith. I'd like to have a real answer to why you wouldn't wait for me to wake up. Afraid I might start to like you?" Megan's playful tone changed slightly. She looked for answers.

Leo hesitated, but satisfied himself that he would answer this embarrassing question or he would walk home. "Maybe I was afraid to wait until you were awake." The only explanation he ever gave. He was off the hook, an anticlimactic end.

Chapter 16
Trenches

Sitting on the edge of his mattress, no longer examining the decrepit space around him, Leo realized the magnitude of his boredom. Aside from a few hoop hours, and time spent with Megan his calendar remained empty. Answers failed to find him in the two days since his trip to Dorie's Cove, and rather than continuing his search, he continued to turn pages, passing the time. The heroine, Dagny, in his latest read, failed to move his mind from the still monumental fact that those closest to him led him astray.

He thought while he scanned each line and constantly, as it had become protocol, found himself confused by the bottom of each page. His eyes focused while his mind wandered elsewhere, thoughts floating back and forth between words like deception and deceit. The deception he could neither confront nor ignore ultimately led him to deceive himself. In forty minutes of morning light he read only four pages and consumed no meaning. The pattern frustrated him. Refusing to let himself concentrate or cope, he finally fired the book across the room into an empty picture frame. The book hit the floor as the frame swung like a pendulum from the single concealed nail. He failed to knock it down.

Leo jumped off his bed onto the ten remaining square feet of floor and began pacing along the creaking planks of slivered wood. Two strides in either direction left him staring at the opposite wall. He turned with his fury, striding in couplets to the other side of the room where he confronted the wall again. The brief emptiness of the room, like the walls, failed to supply him with the adversary he needed. He threw open the bedroom door with the intention of making his feelings known to the first person who would listen. Richard, Megan, Maude, or Margaret Fortun could have been his unknowing target. He sought release, and would take it anywhere. He slammed the door and stared at it from inside his room.

"Why can't I commit?" He screamed it with all his rage and the walls of the cottage shook. The single audible question enabled him to make his decision. He threw open the door again with the concrete determination that he would be heard. With seven paces, he marched to the end of the corridor, the strides feeling like a walk through eternity.

When Leo opened the outside door the look on his face remained placid, though what he saw should have been unfathomable. He calmly stared at the ghost before him. "I think it's time for the two of us to have a talk, Mr. Smith. If you're not busy I think now would be a good time."

Leo stared at a man he knew only as Walden. "I wasn't exactly expecting to see you here. I suppose if I asked what you were doing here, or how you know where I live, you would tell me that it's a small island."

"Probably."

"Actually, I'm on my way to discuss something kind of important with my father. We've had a little difference of opinion in the family and I hope to clear it up."

The look on Walden's face confessed his complete knowledge of Leo's situation. In front of the cottage on a cloudy day, they simply stared at one another refreshed by the assurance that there were no more lies to tell. Leo broke the silence of their impromptu staring match and spoke first. "I suppose you know all about the obstacle course that's been built for poor, helpless Leo." The persuasion in Walden's eyes never altered and his pertinacious stare revealed he knew everything.

"Et tu Brute?"

"No. I wouldn't say that."

"Yes, you would. Since the time I got here you've been looking over my shoulder, giving me advice, spiritual healing crap, and now I find out that you knew about the entire hoax." Leo's face became flushed with anger. "Why didn't you advise me on that. Don't you think that information would have helped master?" Close to divulging all his feelings for the man in front of him to observe, something told him that this hippie, guru tutor played on his team. "Why did you do it?" The one question he would never ask.

The two men started along the footpath passing the hotel and extending toward the harbor. Reaching the last dry rocks of the jetty, Walden motioned for Leo to sit down. Each of his movements disclosed his serious nature, while Leo accepted ignorance, not knowing what this mysterious man would say. Walden stood, not as a man, but as a tower before the Atlantic background filled with meandering ships. The ships completed the scene for the opening of the last act and the one player who now took the stage. As the expression on the man's face changed, Leo anticipated the coming monologue meant not just for him, but for anyone filled with despair. Skeptical and eager, the young student prepared to listen.

"Leo, I can honestly say that I am not one of them. When I say 'one of them' I don't mean your father or mother or a

Miss Fortun." He named all the players except one. "I speak of all those people who lack faith, not just in you, but in life. The reason I didn't come to you earlier is... well I needed to see how you, one individual in all this sunshine, would handle things. I don't waste my time, Leo. I don't believe in it anymore. Your capacity to own your responsibilities drew me to you." Leo lifted his head, prepared to speak, but Walden stopped him with a wave of his hand. "Hear me out, Leo. I think...I know you're interested.

"When I first learned of your situation, I believed many mistakes were being made. At the same time I wondered how I could possibly know what you needed. I knew nothing of you, so I waited. I waited to assess the thunderous character within you, and your rare ability to handle the devastating tragedy in your life. The only person, who truly merits help, Leo, is the one who doesn't need it or ask for it. The person, who doesn't expect everyone else to carry their weight for them, is the person who deserves to have the load taken from their shoulders. The people who made all the decisions for you simply couldn't comprehend your strength. They just don't have it; therefore, they can't see it. They thought they were giving something to you, when in fact they were taking.

"Leo, I look at you and I see a troubled soul rather than a troubled boy. I see what you're thinking by the expression on your face. 'Here we go again with the prescription via Woodstock.' That isn't the case at all. When I say 'soul,' I'm certain I hold the same definition you would. If your heart and your mind can't figure out which one of the two is wrong, the conflict lies in your soul. Your heart believes you should mourn and your mind knows that a great friend would never want you to." Leo flinched, as the lesson became personal. "It's okay, Leo, all the strongest people face these days while all the weakest hide from them.

"People are tested, Leo. It's not just you or just me." Walden paused and looked up toward the low clouds. The impending rain should have begun already, but with good reason it waited patiently. "Everyone has problems, Leo. Tragedy strikes us all. The unfortunate circumstance for you is that you're so equipped to deal with the problem you're stumbling through multiple solutions. It begs one simple question. How will *you* finally resolve the conflict?"

Walden searched around him, paying particular attention to the beach, as if the people along the coastline plotted impatiently to steal his fire. Prometheus gone, his glance became one of contemplation. He began disclosing his secret.

"Let me tell you a story about a man who failed his test, Leo. This guy knew all his life what he wanted to do. He fell in love with Herman Melville, Nathaniel Hawthorne, classics, poetry, and particularly Shakespeare." He chose to divulge his secret early. "All his life he wanted to teach literature, not just teach it, but profess it, to anyone who wanted to learn. He made his dream come true and he screamed poetry, roared prose, and believed in the course of it all that he changed lives. I believe he did. In his classroom, students saw the world of literature as it should be seen. They revered it, until it ended.

"One day a dean of students strolled into his office and passively began screaming bloody murder. A young, inexperienced filly from one of his classes had filed sexual harassment charges against him. To avoid a public, university scandal, a compromise was reached. If the student would drop the charges, the college would have no trouble dropping the professor. No one involved got their hands dirty; not even the suspected perpetrator. If he resigns quietly they won't even put a black mark on his record. He could have secured another teaching job anywhere he wanted with his history of prominence. Trouble is, now his dream is tarnished and he loses his faith. He simply stopped believing in everything he accomplished and anything he ever would. Any guesses who that guy was?"

Leo understood Walden's rhetoric, and awaited the confession certain to follow another brief gaze of Atlantic contemplation. Looking down at the boulders beneath him, then up at the professor in front of him, the young man knew this was not the time for his words. Coupled with the movement of his eyes, he acknowledged Walden with a subtle nod revealing his most immediate thought: "Yes, I know."

"I can't say I've led a hard life since that day. I managed to make one great investment along the way and my only work involves labor of the mind, my favorite kind of work if you hadn't guessed. I have very few regrets, but every once in a while I stand on these rocks and begin a familiar lesson of literature. She listens well." He made the unnecessary gesture of motioning toward the sea, but Leo already grasped the meaning, and the nature of his student.

"I loved those kids, Leo, but that one betrayal broke me. I believed that I couldn't help them anymore." He paused again, while the waves crashed violently over the end of the wall. "I loved that student. Whether the allegations were true never mattered to me, it was my fault.

"The connection isn't between you and I, or even you and the next guy, it's between all of us. All you have to do is sit down with a clear head and serious focus to decide how Leo Smith can pass his test. The 'What now?' is yours alone. Once you really think it out and decide, you'll have done the right thing." Walden turned and started back along the wall toward the beach prepared to disappear again.

Allowing less than ten steps, Leo shouted after him. "And the mistakes?"

Walden had finished but refused to dismiss the question. When he turned back, Leo asked again. "What about the mistakes?"

"The mistakes are the most difficult part." As if it were a prepared speech or a polished soliloquy, Walden continued to orate aloud though Leo knew he was not necessarily speaking to him; his audience always larger. "Somewhere in the deep trenches of my most complex and elementary thoughts, I see with great clarity the person I wanted to be and the canyon of indifference, which separates me from that lost soul I see in the mirror of my best days. Daily, weekly, and monthly I fail to comprehend how the existence of my 'self' and the existence of my goals never converge, and why I accept myself as unaccomplished. In the same breath of that failure, I see success, woven in the fabric of my brothers, my students, my loves, my family, and my vision, yet I'm incomplete. Not the completion sought in life by the poor fool who wants everything, but a complete moment of happiness.

"I've looked for that moment. I haven't journeyed the globe or searched the unscathed corners of my mind, but I've looked continuously in every classroom, library, bookstore, break wall, beach, and ocean I've ever encountered. I've never failed to see what's in front of me, but I've often failed to appreciate it, and therein lies the confusion. It's not the complex labyrinth of turns that keeps me wavering and uncertain, it is the simplicity of my conviction. That is only this: I don't know what I'm looking for any longer, and I feel my eyes closing. I'm settling in, accepting mediocrity, and staring into the dim light of the dark road at the guy preaching to fish, making love to a bottle, rather than a man on a mountaintop, with dreams in his right hand, and reality in his left. What would I say to that man on the mountaintop?"

Unsure if he should answer, Leo held the silence with Walden.

"Clap!

"I'd want him to clap, not in celebration of the mountain climbed, not in celebration of the mountain conceived and devised by an omnipotent power, but simply to watch dreams and reality collide. If I were that man, I would defeat the winds of desperation in that clap because I have faced my fear, and brought these two things together with the force of a thousand thunderbolts hurled like a message from Olympus, and I have brought them together with the softness and silence of a glance exchanged inadvertently in a subway station. But I have brought them together.

"Clap!

"In that moment on a high peak concocted only by searching those deep trenches inside, I could celebrate, not because I've found the goal at the end of the journey, but the goal at the beginning. Standing at the top of that rock where men excited their dreams before me, I would do what could only come naturally at the top of the world in my time of exultation. I'd go up.

"I would not elevate because there was a next goal, I would not ascend to shock and defy the laws of physics, I would rise because I've done it before. In my most immediate past I found the invisible, metaphysical clash of opposites and brought them together, having done it once, I would easily and painlessly do it again. The goal I failed to see becomes realized without the predetermined method of consulting my senses, and now when I close my eyes, I see.

"I fear, however, that is not for me. I cannot reach the top because I've ceased climbing and begun my reality on a jetty where I can plan my words and invent solutions. My mountain of existentialist meanings is circumvented because I've stopped staring it in the face. Fate rests squarely on the shoulders of those who seek it, grab hold of it in a death squeeze, and embrace it like their truest love. We make our luck. We choose our own lot. We write our own Bardian histories, tragedies, and comedies. We allow and dismiss the clichés of the every day while we dismiss and allow the exuberance of original thought high on the mountain of deep trenches. I have exhausted my options, because I consider too many in the random scattering of my talking, and more importantly, my breathing, as I seek perfection, without working hard enough to achieve it. Two steps from clinical depression and an ounce on the scale from unrelenting joy and adulation of life, I reveal my existence to the rocks.

"But are there revelations? If so, I would storm off this wall, grab the balls of 'life rules,' climb a mountain, sneer at the countenance of life, and mash my dreams and reality into a pulp. A juicy, bloody, ubiquitous, ball of hope, and from that ball I would begin, like a Big Bang, to create my universe.

"But I couldn't just stare and begin. I would question the mountaintop, wondering if I had made a mistake. And alas, there's the difference. I have not climbed a step, stretched my dreams, or kicked fate squarely in the chin and already I seek the inadequacy of the moment. And there is the solution. I have found the overwhelming pessimism that pervades my thoughts and proceeds my actions to the festival of constructive ideation. Complete happiness is a farce in my world of 'what ifs' and 'one-step-aways' because I ponder. There are no answers in the deep trenches; there are only monkey wrenches waiting to defenestrate themselves through the windows of the answers I already know, and the decisions I have already made.

"The inadequacies are not the problem, they are the solution. Finding happiness rather than indifference in those inadequacies and mistakes is the golden key to the gates of success. You have to love the wrenches as much as you love the windows they break. Whether the pane of an idea is broken or not the light will still shine through. In that light, you will see yourself most clearly." He turned back to the beach and walked away. Finally, speaking to Leo again, he uttered a last sentence sounding like the echoing cry of a wounded animal more than the solution to a young man's problems. "In the light of your mistakes."

Leo sat on the wall, as a picture of serenity, digesting the last words of a ghost. He realized he could not let this man leave without one last question. "Walden," he yelled to the professor of waves. He turned back a last time and faced Leo. "I promise I'll make the decision on my own, but I have to ask. What would you do?"

There was the slightest hint of a smile on his face and Leo could not understand why until the teacher answered, and it became evident. "Don't ask me. I failed." He turned and resumed his stride.

In the next few hours, Leo lost himself within his own thoughts. Each hour seemed to pass with every wave that broke along the wall and in the meantime the unfriendly clouds finally broke letting the omnipotent rays of sunlight spear through. The holes in the sky gave Leo a sense of things infinite. For the first time since the death, Leo could feel real faith in the decisions he made. The lesson.

So many years removed from his own lesson Walden dodged humility, able to deliver those last two important words: "I failed." The man who failed to keep teaching taught Leo well in the most intimate trenches. Leo moved along the break wall in the same direction of Walden more than three hours ago. He understood his last lesson, only the execution remained.

Craving continued exposure to the outdoors, Leo began a bicycle ride toward the north end of the island noticing the exquisite landscape as he pedaled. There were no trees anywhere on the entire four-mile stretch of road, and the small shrubs along the sides of the asphalt were nonexistent compared to the woods he recalled from home. They were a blanket, rather than a curtain covering the scenery around him. Leo rode two miles before he noticed the absence of any hills on this road, and he wondered if the glaciers that built this island had any imagination at all. Remembering the bluffs, he silently apologized. He searched for natural landmarks to define one spot from any other, but found nothing thinking the north side of this postage stamp in the Atlantic enjoyed no character worth mentioning. Suddenly he realized his mistake. This stretch of shoreline united, one square mile never yielding to the next, only blending with it. Parts of the island came together from thousands of miles away and merged together indiscriminately. He imagined people doing the same, and then laughed at his own fiction. The land had no ego.

More and more along the course of his revitalizing path, he relied on his thoughts to pass the time, and sometimes the anguish. He stared vacantly at the North Lighthouse when he reached the end of the road where it met the sea. He leaned the bicycle against his hip and stared out over the clear horizon that threatened powerfully a few hours ago. The sun dropped steadily, ready to converge with the new horizon, and an orange filter altered the color of the world. Discerning that he could never reach that filter, the rest of the world became tangible. The magnificence of the lighthouse did not merit a second glance as the surrounding earth overshadowed any of man's most brilliant accomplishments. While the chiseled stone served as an island attraction, Leo thought only of how it detracted from the excellence of the landscape.

As quickly as it had come, the orange disappeared, replaced by the purple haze stretching over the island and beyond. The meeting of the sun and the horizon supplied the awe Leo sought on this brief trip, and at last the line of the land won another night game. Leo felt comfort in the knowledge that the show would run again tomorrow.

The moon had not taken its position in the sky so Leo rode south dodging the darkness. Sequestered island life became as obvious as ever, but Leo secured himself with the wisdom that life was better. He would sleep well knowing that Walden would not give up teaching and the sun would not stop setting.

Chapter 17
Riley

The loud, unexpected knock shot through him like a freshly sharpened knife, and he staggered down the hall to the outside door uncertain of who would surprise him this time. He opened the door to an explosion of morning sunlight and gawked in surprise at the slender woman who stood before him. Framed by the chipped paint and backed by gifts of nature, she looked like she belonged on his doorstep, more than anywhere else in the world.

"Good morning, sunshine," she said.

"Good morning." Leo, not yet completely awake, unintentionally contained the pleasure he felt in seeing her. "I hope you don't take this the wrong way, but what are you doing here?"

"Don't worry," she brought relief in the same contagious way she always did. "I know you weren't expecting an early morning wake up call but I just wanted to come by and tell you not to be late for work tonight."

Under the original circumstances Leo would have assumed his father fell in love with the bottle again, but with their secret exposed, he understood no danger remained. Megan's face held the expression of a third grader with a secret dying to call out, "I know something you don't know." Leo asked politely, "What the hell are you talking about?"

"I know you're enjoying the life of Riley out here, but you have to be a little bored. I figure you might be interested in a job. The owner called the bar last night, and told me to hire another bartender. You're my guy."

Leo remained perplexed. "Megan, I don't really even drink, what do I know about being a bartender?"

"That's the beauty of it. You don't have to know anything. He said he wanted a bar back for my shifts because I'm normally swamped. You make the gin and tonics and stock the refrigerators. I'll make all the hard drinks. You can pour beer, can't you?"

"I still don't understand. Every single person on this island has to be more qualified than I am. Why would he want to hire me?"

"He doesn't have to hire you. I do. He specifically said for me to do the hiring. It was really weird. He practically described you over the phone when he told me who he wanted." Leo's confusion turned to excitement thinking that work at O'Mally's allowed him to have the one thing he wanted most; more time with Megan. Perfect.

"So when do I meet this owner who thinks I'm the ideal employee."

The peculiar look on Megan's face forewarned Leo of the rather unusual answer that followed. "To tell you the truth, Leo, you'll probably never meet him. I've been working here a few years now and I've never met the guy myself. All our checks come in the mail. We make the night deposits, and as you already know, we do the hiring. He must live on the mainland because no one seems to know O'Mally, or if there is an O'Mally. No one ever gets fired because we always pick people that we want to work with. It's probably a lot like picking teams in basketball. You don't want anyone who hurts the team." Megan shrugged her shoulders letting Leo know that the owner would remain a mystery.

"So you pick me."

"Yes, I pick you."

"What time do I start?"

"I'll swing by around six. You can start right after I take you out for dinner." Anxiety hovered thick in the air, and they could only define their own continuing uncertainty in this summer of new experience. "And, Leo, take a shower. You stink."

"That's twice. I'm getting a complex." Megan walked away through the path of Leo's vision and he enjoyed every step until she turned the corner and moved out of sight. The trickery surrounding his junket to the island no longer lived in the forefront of his mind as it did for the past dangerous day. In the next few hours, he would think only of Megan.

Dinner proceeded as a brief engagement between two inquisitive children testing the ice on a newly frozen pond. The porch of the Steamship Restaurant welcomed both the elegant and the everyday in a manner mirroring the island. Some couples wore shirts with ties and sundresses while others wore staff shirts for O'Mally's pub and baseball hats. Dinner conversation for the latter couple wandered from movies, to magazines, and even included a few unamusing jokes. Neither of them offered anything truly intimate, nor did they ask. Leo, young and inexperienced, labored through his meal afraid to say anything foolish. Megan, mature and confident, feared the same. They survived dinner by communicating throughout the whole meal without ever really talking. Leo logged one mental note in his mind to never order linguini with red sauce on a date again, and Megan allowed him to forget the comedy.

They walked in the back door of O'Mally's just before eight o'clock and Megan used the extra minutes before her shift to show Leo where he could find glasses, ice, kegs, and anything else important. Carrying ice and pouring beers is less than demanding labor, and Leo enjoyed the prospect of keeping busy.

"What did I tell you, Leo? Nothing could be easier. If you screw up nobody screams and the work gets easier by the hour. Tom's getting ready to go, so we're up." They moved from the storage room in the back, toward the bar and even this seemed like a great place to spend time together. "Hey, Tom, this is Leo. He starts tonight."

Tom's blond hair, tan skin, and good looks made him a poster child for any beach looking to draw a crowd, but far less than intimidating, he could not have appeared more harmless. His emerald -green eyes conveyed kindness the way words rarely do. "Good luck, Leo. Should be a piece of cake." Harmless. "By the way UPS dropped a package for you. It's behind the bar."

"Thanks." Tom walked through the back and out the door. "Seems like a nice guy."

Megan searched for the package behind the bar. "I wonder who sent you a package. Do you have any idea?"

"No." Leo looked around the bar preoccupied with the prospect of a new job, another new experience. Two old men sat at the end of the mahogany and showed no signs of life while their full beers floated on deep rings of perspiration circling the bottoms of the glasses. Looking less like customers and more like permanence, the men scarcely breathed, and never drank from the mugs in front of them.

"It feels like a book." Megan found the package. Leo hardly noticed her, a very rare occasion.

Leo opened the neatly wrapped package exposing a thin, leather bound journal. The hunter green cover met the gold leafed pages without contrast. Leo found nothing within to indicate who the purchased the present. The inscription on the first page read: “IMITATION IS SUICIDE. Go well.” Leo reminded himself of why he journeyed to the island, and accepted that every painful emotion he thought he wanted to forget would be saved in ink. He said what came to his mind first. “It’s perfect.”

“You ready to set up for the evening crowd?”

“Thanks, Megan. This was really thoughtful of you.”

“Judging by your reaction I wish I’d thought of it. Whoever sent it sure knew what you wanted.” He did.

Over the course of the evening, the bar entertained the usual menagerie of characters safer in the confines of the bar than the peaceful streets. Loud, obnoxious tourists and frustrated locals packed the pub until tempers flared, and glasses broke. Megan’s patience and Leo’s determination enabled them to struggle through their first night as coworkers. When the bar closed, they were reminded of the night’s chaos by the orchards of empty and half-empty, glasses and bottles scattered across the bar. The floor, comprised of cigarette butts rather than tile, signaled a reminder that a lot of work remained.

“Shall we review?” Megan always cherished the calm after the storm but on this night she permeated more excitement than usual. “Within the course of this evening you broke up a potential bar brawl because one guy called another guy’s wife fat, and then almost started a brawl because the same guy grabbed my ass while I grabbed ice.”

“Well he deser...”

“I’m not finished yet,” she interjected. “Let’s talk about the ‘sombrero’ incident. I told you if you had any questions about drinks you only had to ask me, but you decided you’d fix it all on your own. After referencing all three of the bartender guides we have, you come up empty. Kahluha and milk, there's a tough drink. Three spilled beers, two broken glasses..."

"And a partridge in a pear tree. Just remember this whole thing was your idea." Leo, flustered by Megan's taunting, allowed his male ego to show.

Megan decided the hour arrived to let her coworker in on the secret. "Leo, the first night I worked here was a busy night just like always this time of the season. I was starting as a cocktail waitress and not only did I drop an entire tray, my mystery drink was sloe gin. Five minutes trying to make s-l-o-w gin. This place has never seen anything but beginners. I guess the owner just likes new employees to take their lumps so everyone works their way up and no one comes off as a big shot. Every person who's ever worked here had a tough first night. He wants students."

Chapter 18
Waiting

Young Mr. Smith spent the next week on a small island enjoying a relaxing schedule all perpetuated by the deceit of his loved ones. He worked five of the previous six nights, slept late most mornings, played basketball every afternoon, and spent every possible free moment with Megan. Walks on Main Street were filled with greetings from residents he knew, and tourists who visited O'Mally's. Everyone remembers the friendly bartender who buys his patrons a round and doubles his tips. They always remember, even in the course of a single week. He still ate dinner with the Fortun's at night, and twice stopped to see his father laboring through the night watch when he walked home from work. They spoke in a manner most accurately described as cordial and Leo never disclosed his knowledge of the secret plan they devised. Instead of dreading time spent on the island, he believed he would miss it in the near future. Specifically, he would miss Megan. Their physical relationship never progressed beyond the one innocent kiss they shared on the beach, but they inevitably became great friends. Thoughts of their separation therefore, were unavoidable.

Leo often wondered what became of Walden. He lived invisibly on the island since their last tutorial session on the break wall. Leo remembered his preparation to disclose secret knowledge and desert the island on the incongruous day Walden appeared at his door. He realized daily what a terrible mistake he nearly made. In the past week he spent many hours on the jetty waiting for his vociferous friend to return, but he never did. Each night when he left work, he expected to see Walden on the street poised to deliver a lesson, or completely inebriated, anxious to shine shoes. Nothing. Leo failed to recognize that he currently lived immersed in a lesson. He was learning to stand, alone.

"Hey, pal, what's a guy have to do to get a martini around here?" Typical, obnoxious behavior.

"Order a martini," Leo responded.

"Very funny. Don't thin it out with all that Vermouth crap either."

"Gin or Vodka?"

"Vodka. For Christ's sakes, who drinks gin?"

"What's the matter, pal, you have a tough day or something?"

"Who are you, Dear Abbey?"

"Listen friend, if you don't want to talk about it that's fine. It's just that sometimes people unload their problems on bartenders so I figured maybe you wanted to do the same." Leo put the vodka back on the shelf. "I won't mention it again. If the martini isn't dry enough, let me know."

"How much do I owe you?"

"First one is on me." Leo walked away from the dismayed man and continued stocking the bar.

The man leaning over the brass rail nursed his martini and looked ready to talk. The twenty-five-year-old appeared closer to thirty-five, hanging his head at the end of the bar under a weight more significant than gravity. Suddenly, he got up from his stool and walked out of the room. Leo picked up the five-dollar tip the man left while thinking back to his first day in O'Mally's. He knew he looked a lot like the man who just abandoned the building, and forced himself to accept the circles of life spinning men with a lot on their minds. He secretly wondered if Walden waited outside for the man, ready to dissect his character and explain clandestine solutions. The thought made him smile.

Busy bringing bottled beers from the cooler to the ice chest, he failed to see her come in. "Hey can't a lady get a drink around here." Megan arrived two hours early for work.

"What are you doing here?"

"I hope you don't mind but I can't work tonight. Do you think you can handle it by yourself?"

"Yeah, but why aren't you coming in. Is everything all right?" Genuine concern sounded obvious in his voice.

"Everything is fine. I can stay until ten if you want a few hours off."

"No, don't worry about it. Do you want a drink?"

"Beer."

"Woman after my own heart," said Leo.

"You don't even drink," she returned.

"What's drinking have to do with it?"

Leo poured her a beer. Boring by his pouring standards, the Amstel Light represented the only alcohol Megan ever drank.

They talked for a while about miserable customers and free afternoons while a few patrons entered the bar. Finally, Leo asked a question he would soon regret, "So if everything is okay why aren't you coming into work tonight?" Megan usually appeared early and excited for work in their week together; no long stretch in the real world, but decent compared to many island workers. Contrary to the most popular modern opinions about work, this woman loved her job.

"I have a date." Megan answered without any guilt or even the slightest sign of disclosing something she would rather not. She stated her evening plans as a matter of fact, not as the arrow through Leo's heart.

The bartender attempted to maintain his composure by responding quickly. He hesitated just long enough to remove the arrow and spoke. "A big date, huh? Well I'm sure it's been a while since you've been out, you'd better go and get ready." Transparent in his stealthy effort at indifference, they both recognized his futility and Megan's expression now conveyed understanding.

"Leo, does it bother you that I'm going on a date? If it bothers you, I can cancel it." *Cancel it*, he screamed without making a noise, and once again she grasped the reigns. Just as Leo accepted the humiliation of Megan's revelation, something worse happened.

"All right, as long as you're sure you don't need any help I guess I'll take off." Impossible. She was the rock, always there for him, until now.

The Thursday night crowd seeped in the door slowly, as usual, and Leo gazed at the stagnant arms of the clock taunting nine-thirty. He poured five beers in the last fifteen minutes and begged for something to do. His begging ceased when Tom walked through the door in work clothes. Leo would have loved to dump the shift but his morality deemed it cruel and unusual. "Thanks, buddy, but we're dead tonight. You don't need to be here."

"I thought you had to leave." Tom and Leo were equally bewildered. "I got a message from one of my roommates that you were off at ten, and needed someone to cover."

"I didn't leave it."

"I know he said that..."

"Maybe I can explain." The voice came from the storage area and by the time Tom could see her face, Leo already knew. She sauntered in the back door unnoticed, and eagerly awaited the opportunity to resolve the chaos. "You know, Leo, this isn't very flattering. It couldn't have been more than a couple of hours ago when I asked you for a date and you've forgotten already. You sure know how to make a girl feel good about herself." Leo cursed under his breath, hanging his head, seeking a happy place, remembering how jealous he became when Megan explained her reason for missing work.

"How could I have been so stupid? Was that tonight?" Hook, line, and sinker, he knew there would be no recovery.

"Now, Leo, when you say you feel stupid, do you mean you feel stupid because you forgot so quickly, or you feel stupid because you thought I meant I had a date with someone other than you."

"Let's go." Leo wanted desperately to avoid a new segment of abuse if Tom discovered the basis of this odd conversation. "Thanks a lot, Tom," Leo said before he escorted Megan out the door.

The two bartenders walked along the comfortable sidewalk past Megan's car before Leo's curiosity became words. "So, where are we headed this time?" Noticing the unusually quiet street, Megan enjoyed the sound of Leo's voice in the night air.

"I think at least one of us needs to change our clothes. I can't have my date out on the town in the clothes he wore to work." Megan's humor proliferated itself from the seed of jealousy she planted in Leo's mind, and she ignored the temptation to tell him he needed another shower. He enjoyed her games; he was sure of it.

"Does that mean you're coming over to watch me get undressed? You little tramp."

"I'm sorry. If you're ashamed or embarrassed, I could wait by the car." Incessant. She glanced downward conducting a mock inspection of Leo's body and the transparent gesture succeeded in making her date nervous. "But what fun would that be," she added.

The couple walked across the street and through The Grand parking lot to the cottage. Entering Leo's room, more tension and hesitation surfaced than ever before, because there are natural steps and these two were bounding upward. "Do you want me to wait in the hall while you change?"

"Actually, if you're not in too much of a rush I figured I'd take a shower. Couldn't deal with you telling me I stink again." In the faint light of his room filled with marvelous energy, Leo observed Megan completely. She wore a silk blouse with a long, dark, sheer skirt. The floral print represented a formal and informal intention, indicating her preparation for anything. Her jewelry, a bit more flashy than usual, caught the dim light and reflected the perfection of the wearer. "Should I assume we're going somewhere nice or are you just trying harder than usual to impress me."

Leo expected the usual barrage of retaliatory comments from Megan, but she instead sat quietly on the edge of his bed. She rarely lacked a witty response so Leo knew her mind drifted elsewhere. Instead of humor, he relied on his actual thoughts. "You look great." It could have been a useless comment uttered a million times by a million men, but the simplicity magnified his honesty, and for a few beats of her accelerating heart she looked away from him. The words were a firm handshake rather than a wet kiss and that difference gave his words the meaning she would accept. Silence enveloped the room while they both adjusted to the first compliment of the evening. The reliable creak of floorboards broke the silence when Leo moved to the closet retrieving a towel. He stole one last look at the wonderful woman in his room before he stepped out into the hall and safety.

Leo guessed that every person endures times when they want, more than anything, to read the mind of another. Invading the thoughts and stealing the secrets of another person's mind could erase all the worry of a dumbfounded young man. Leo wished for that power as he felt the water hitting his body, and then thanked God for goose bumps and no special gifts.

He stepped out from the shower sensing he would be the one to make the first move, he would show his emotions first in the tireless chess match their friendship had become. He sensed the necessary time arrived to take Megan in his arms and allow his fiery emotions to pour over her. Then he sensed his clothes were missing. He thought of Megan relaxing in his room passively waiting for him to make the lavish entrance he prepared so well under the flow of the forgiving water. "Are there great entrances," he wondered, "by men in towels?"

Left with only one option, Leo struggled toward his room. He stopped at the door taking one last deep breath before he entered his room hesitantly. Looking in the door as it opened, he saw the pants he brought to the bathroom folded on the edge of his bed. His confusion halted when his eyes moved forward fearfully and he saw her at the foot of his bed wearing the oxford shirt he carried down the hall. His former bewilderment became unyielding disbelief when he noticed she wore nothing else.

"Like my shirt?" Megan smiled. Leo froze.

The expression of hand-grenades and heart attacks on Leo's face forced Megan to consider that she made a mistake. She expected a warm tackle, and an end to a long wait, when he entered the room. He stood motionless. She expected a sigh of relief. He was not breathing. "I'm sorry Leo. I thought we could both see this coming." She broke eye contact with him and seemed to cover herself without ever moving. "I thought we both wanted this."

Standing in a room with the beautiful woman he thought about every day since their first meeting, he felt completely alone with his inferiority. The growing emotions he knew since his first day on the island collapsed into nothing. In that moment, he could only hear the deafening thunder of the useless question booming through a bullhorn in his mind. *What do I do?*

"Would it be better if I left?"

Leo did not answer. Megan slowly moved off the bed, walked across the room, and stood facing Leo. She leaned in close to him, looking past his eyes and into his mind, until their faces were only inches apart. Everything he failed to say in complex, confusing sentences now belonged to her with those few steps across the room serving as proof of ownership. She understood. She kissed him with a rushing flood of exhilaration that dammed itself in their friendship. The wall of inexperience melted away in the heat, and Leo returned her kiss. Reality and dreams collide on the mountain of deep trenches. This dream lived in the deepest parts of his own mind and he dove to reach it.

In one single movement, without either of them maneuvering the other, they fell onto the bed. Inevitably, Leo moved sheepishly through the first sexual experience of his life. Nervous and clumsy, as seventeen-year-old boys tend to be, he needed sensitive coaching. Without words, Megan moved his body in rhythm with hers as they floated through togetherness knowing details would be forgotten. They were coworkers striving towards the other person's goal. He removed his shirt from her warm, willing, golden body with comfortable ease, while she slid the towel from his waist. Exploring their naked bodies, each of them, adjusted, moved, touched, and kissed carefully, considering the pleasure of the other in a rare partnership of selflessness. Immense cries of gratification did not escape their lips, romance novels would not be written, but in a small, dilapidated room on an obscure island, they shared a completely spiritual act. They hardly noticed the sex.

"So now am I supposed to smoke a cigarette?" Leo broke their rhythm falling back to the pillow.

"Only if you can catch your breath."

"Then maybe I'd better wait." Megan rolled onto his body and rested her head on his chest playfully. She could feel the words come through his body when he added, "until tomorrow." Closing his eyes, he kissed her on the forehead trying to immortalize the moment in his mind. He did. Then, in perhaps a more intimate way, they fell asleep together.

Megan awoke staring into the red lines of the clock. "1:15 a.m." She attempted to slide out of the bed without waking Leo, but he noticed the movements of her body as if it were his own.

"Where do you think you're going?" His voice remained weak from their slumber but his arms gripped her firmly, holding her in place.

"O'Mally's. I'm sure Tom could use some help closing up. I figure it's the least I can do since I took the whole night off and stole the other bartender." She made a weak effort to move away from him.

"I've got a better idea. You stay right here. I'll go clean up and then I'll have something to look forward to when I get back." Leo grinned conveying his intentions.

"Why, Mr. Smith, if I didn't know any better I'd think you were making some sort of indecent suggestion to me. I'm not sure a proper lady could accept such an offer."

"Thank God you're not a lady." Leo slid out from under the wrinkled white sheets while Megan held her spot. Neither emerged willing to say it directly, but the idea of reenacting the night appealed to them both. Delighted with his gentle kiss on her cheek, she pulled the covers to her shoulders and actually giggled when he left the room. Youth is contagious, especially among the young.

Leo's carefree whistle could be heard over the crashing waves as he walked from the hotel toward O'Mally's. For the first time in a long succession of stumbling, a few brief hours worked out exactly the way he wanted. He inhaled those hours in life when a small move in the right direction sent him down an unchartered path. The path was Megan. She was direction.

Tom sat alone in the vacant bar in the corner booth counting out his tips. The emptiness felt good to Leo when he noticed a small picture of the North Light on the wall. He never noticed it before. Tom looked toward him prepared to tell a prospective patron the bar closed for the night. "I thought you were a townie looking for a late last call. What are you doing back here, kid?" Tom called everyone "kid."

"I figured since I left you for dead, I'd come back and close up for you."

"Don't worry about it, kid. We got a late rush and I made a bundle in tips. That always puts me in a good mood so I don't mind closing her down. I'm glad you left me." He paused to consider Leo's presence. "I hope you didn't screw things up with Megan just to come back here and mop floors." Tom chuckled at the idea of Leo choosing the bar over Megan.

"No, somehow I don't think I screwed anything up." Fierce pride.

"Good. Then do me a favor and get out of here. You know I love the glory work. If I didn't have barsludged floors and errant urinal shots to clean, who would I be?" Tom waved to Leo and returned his attention to counting money. He was a good guy unprepared to take life too seriously, one of those precious few people who are occasionally hated because nothing ever gets them down. People envied the quality. Leo walked back out on to the street.

"Excuse me. This is a private throughway." Leo turned to match a face with the unfamiliar voice echoing behind him. The Grand Hotel night watchman, about to continue speaking, recognized his son. Trapped in the tragedy of the situation, the Smith men stared at one another, a father and son. They were a father who did not recognize the sight of his own son, and a son who did not recognize the voice of his own father. Hesitating, neither of them broke the silence, entertaining the same thoughts, wondering what a bloodline meant to a person you don't even know.

"What are you doing out here so late?" Richard finally broke the tension.

"I'm on my way to bed."

"Were you working late at O'Mally's?"

"Not exactly. What are you doing out here?"

"Just making the rounds." The two men could have been from different planets. Each of them lacked all understanding as to what the other might be thinking, and their small talk represented an icy segue to nowhere. They stood together in the parking lot miles apart. Leo could have never prepared himself for what came next.

"Do you love me, Leo?" The small talk was quickly and finally over. Richard asked the question with all the emotion his aching heart could create. Leo stood tall in the deserted lot wondering if Richard had actually spoken. This sentimental full house left him contemplative. *How could I possibly love a man I hardly know?* The faint possibility that paternal love could be innate crossed his mind, but passed quickly. He called on all the honesty within him and clung to the most common phrase a seventeen-year-old knows. "I don't know."

Richard Smith's face turned a phantasmal white when he did not hear the frantic, "Yes! Yes! Yes!" he yearned for. He craved forgiveness from the boy he deserted since the desolate day they separated, and now asked it of the man before him. Leo understood that "no" may have been easier for Richard to handle in the darkness of the throughway because recoiling with spite would have been easier than accepting his son's indecisiveness

"I guess that settles things between us." Richard's voice cracked holding back his emotions. "I'm sorry your mother and I lied to you." Leo, surprised that his father knew the surreptitious plan had been exposed to him, showed no change in his countenance, again he never flinched "As I see it now, it was the wrong thing to do. There is something your mother never knew, Leo. I really did need you. I didn't need help battling booze, but I needed to see my son. That much, and my intentions, were true." Richard called upon every muscle in his body to hold back his tears, the way men often do, and this time he managed successfully. "So many mistakes."

A defeated man crumpled before his son. He helped bring Leo into the world, but he would never have him back in his life. Leo felt pity and even sympathy for his father, but neither of those emotions forced the next thing he said. His inspiration surfaced from the echo of Walden in response to his last question, *And what about the mistakes?* "Maybe I want to find out."

"What?"

"I said I don't know if I love you, but I want to find out." Leo's words scraped past the vacancy in his throat where the swelling lump should have been and reached his father's receptive ears. Finally, the tension subsided, and they were men. Leo and Richard Smith sat beside one another on an asphalt curb in the parking lot of The Grand Hotel in the town of New Shoreham, Rhode Island, and began to talk. They never spoke of old times or future dreams. They spoke of basketball players, and recited blonde jokes. Walls crumbled while their conversation continued, and they began to laugh, not as a father and son, but as friends. The only feasible solution to the maturing problem.

An hour escaped them before Richard felt comfortable bringing up their past. He made a simple facetious remark, like many others they shared, but he feared it might be dangerous knowing it served as a reminder for time missed. "So I guess you're a little too old for me to tell you about the birds and the bees." The immediate tension obvious in Leo's body forced Richard to feel he went too far. He would never understand why Leo left him that night and his son would never understand how he forgot about Megan. He sifted through an hour of meaningless conversation with his biological father while a diamond awaited him in the rough. "Listen, I'll talk to you tomorrow. I forgot about something in my room. Thanks for the conversation, Dad." The title held them still for a second before Leo slipped away and Richard fed off the sustenance he long-awaited. Leo never thought of it again.

Jogging through his bedroom doorway, Leo acknowledged the emptiness of the room with a brief, painful sigh. The folded, white sheet of paper, hooded by withered blankets and apprehension, controlled his strides. He wanted nothing less than to open the excruciating letter and read the last words of the woman he deserted. With each written word Leo understood further how he underestimated Megan. She continued to alter his life each day he spent on the island and for the first time in two weeks he heard compassion as he read her note aloud.

"I swear I wasn't eavesdropping. I was on my way to O'Mally's to find you and I saw you talking. The hard parts are behind you, Leo. You're almost home. I'll see you tomorrow." The last three words attacked his heart. *"With love, Megan."*

Chapter 19
Tomorrow

The first rays of daylight struck the world before Leo finally drifted into a deep, comfortable sleep. In the course of his seven-hour slumber the smile never left his face. Unfortunately for Richard, it was not his father who delivered the happiness to his dreams, but the thought of holding the same beautiful woman all over again.

High tide forced the waves into the break wall, sending a mist from the Atlantic Ocean high into the air, before it sprayed downward into Block Island Harbor. The threatening weather never delivered the promised rains, but left an unmistakable reminder in the rough sea. The spray descended onto Leo's journal as he recorded the events of the previous night. Each time he turned a page he could see the impressions of the pen on the next. The record of his past altered his future. The imprints on the blank page asked softly: "Should I love him?" The question was answered on the same coastline where he resolved so many other conflicts. In the ninety-degree heat, through falling mists on the wary boulders, Leo confirmed it. "No, I should not."

He forgave his father and even enjoyed the hour they shared in the early morning, but he could not love him. He decided events such as innate love did not exist, the emotion is learned, and, of course, earned. Staring across the clear horizon, he could see the mainland eight miles away and answers in the haze between. Sound sleep aided him with those answers, and when he awoke three hours earlier he decided to go home based on an undeniable need, without ignoring the one reason to stay. Troubling for so long, the decision in it's finality felt simple, because it belonged only to him.

His pen touched the page of his journal. *One more step. There are no more questions on this journey*. In capital letters three lines high he wrote the word *YES*.

"Perhaps he has learned something after all." Leo was startled by the voice so close behind him, but sitting on those rocks he recognized it immediately.

"Why do you insist on sneaking up on me all the time?"

"I did not *sneak up on you*, you simply failed to hear me approach. All perspective my boy. Thoughts are a very powerful distraction." Leo knew the professor was right again. This habit, like his unannounced entrances, frustrated Leo.

"I'm going home," Leo said.

"Have you decided exactly where that is for you?"

Leo looked down at the last entry in his journal as he answered Walden. "Yes, I have." He never explained his discovery, but Walden understood the young man finally found his way. Even as a wave crashed into the wall and drenched his back, he sat motionless, full of knowledge, and content with his discoveries. In the middle of those barren rocks guarding the harbor, Leo smelled roses.

"Look at the water rolling down the rocks into the harbor." Leo listened, and watched intently as the water slithered down the damp surface. "Think of the time the water spends in the tumultuous Atlantic until it is finally forced over the wall into the calm." The horn sounded on the outgoing ferry. "The water can be forced into the harbor or it can go around the wall and find the calm on it's own. Eventually it reaches tranquillity." They both stared into the ocean.

"Walden." Leo did not prepare a question or seek attention; he said the man's name as a statement to let the world know he could exist.

"I'll see you tomorrow." The professor moved away in huge, unstoppable strides leaving his student alone in the classroom again. Walden blew through like the wind and people would never notice such a man unless they felt him. Leo thought it easier to believe he simply washed up on the welcoming beach and became part of the scenery, than to recognize we could all be like him. His stride stretched as an idea coming to fruition and his words came from a lifetime of looking. As he stood on the wall that day his student never looked at him once. "If this is a man who has failed..." he thought.

"Miss Fortun?" She sat in the kitchen absorbing the flashy photographs of *People* magazine. The gray light in the room drowned out the articles and she strained to see the stars. Leo waited for her to look away from the magazine before informing her he would leave the next day.

"That's nice, Leo." They were the only words she uttered before refocusing on the dark pages in front of her. A businesswoman spoke to him in that kitchen. She knew the easy way.

"Thank you," he said, "for your help."

Their subtle closure ended for Leo when he walked through the kitchen and out onto the lawn. Not until she heard the outside door close did she look up from the stars, and offer her last words. "You'll be fine," she said. And then Maude Fortun began clearing the table.

The desperate search lasted through the afternoon and into the evening as the woman, who helped him the most, ceased to exist on a small, Atlantic island. Leo never found his first love in the few short, painful hours that remained in the brief venture of a lifetime, the trip he would never forget, the ceaseless pain he would never outgrow. Perhaps, an unexpected rush of timidity caught Megan off guard between bursts of her typical, powerful, undeniable strength, and she could not bear to see him go. The possibility charged through Leo's mind that he was a pet project, and with the finish line nearing, she was through with him. His tender ego found no answers for her inexplicable disappearance, and he could not find Megan in the smallest of worlds. Her intentions in refusing to say goodbye remained unclear, but her intentions to help a frightened young man lived immortally in his Leo's mind. His last night would have to pass without her.

Chapter 20
Home

Although the ferry did not depart until nine-thirty on that last, warm, summer morning, Leo's bags were packed two-and-a-half hours earlier. When he closed the door of the cottage, he closed the door on a small, important part of his life, and on a few wonderful people who helped him. There were still two people he needed to thank, and he feared he would only see one of them. Walden would not allow him to depart without a final lesson, but he cringed thinking Megan might let him go. He wished only to see her face one more time before she became a significant part of his past.

Leo felt the temptation to walk out onto the jetty as he descended toward the harbor, but realized his classroom had closed; he had locked it himself. He stood on the small, sandy beach along the edge of the harbor and thought about home. The sun, now ninety minutes high, cleared a path across the ocean and stopped ten feet in front of him where water met land. The ringing in his ears became more audible in the silence of the morning. His mind, like the ocean, was calm.

A child passed him, giggling as he walked up the rocks onto the break wall. Leo watched his agile steps as he jumped from rock to rock moving out over the ocean. The child finally stopped where the wall turned slightly to the east, and the sun embraced him. He appeared angelic as the sunlight engulfed him creeping up into the sky. The nine-year-old boy took two quick steps and plunged headfirst into the sea. He exploded through the surface of the water and climbed the rocks only to turn and dive again. The two rock walls of the harbor formed a giant pool the child claimed as his own. The springless diving board of boulders served as his happiness, and each dive appeared more graceful than the next until it happened, as Leo watched in horror.

The distance between them erased the violent sound of the innocent child colliding with the partially submerged rock. In those first three seconds, Leo already climbed quickly up the rocks onto the jetty. With two steps, he met a full sprint chasing time along the wall. He could see the boy's body settling under the water as he took his last stride across the boulders. With a simple, acrobatic move he dove through the air and crashed through the integrity of the surface of the sea. The chill of the cold splash invigorated his body, heightening his senses and he exercised the swiftest and most effortless movements of his life.

Adrenaline and fear combined to help him move rapidly through the water. He lifted the boy's eighty-five-pound body to the side of the wall and up onto the rocks. He experienced no stimulation in his short life like that filling his body upon seeing the boy's chest move with each breath.

"I called the ambulance." The shout came from the beach. Leo looked at the unconscious boy and the tiny pool of blood forming on the rocks behind his head. Believing the boy escaped any further danger; Leo vomited on the rocks and collapsed beside the child. The man who shouted from the beach approached unnoticed and stood over the dazed youth. "I saw you pulling him up," he said. Leo wondered if there was anything Walden did not see. “He’s still breathing and the cut isn’t very deep. He’ll be fine.”

“I know.” His lungs gulped rapacious breaths and the two frail words were not audible. Then *we* understood together that this journey ended and *mine* could begin.

“What?”

Chapter 21
Voice

"I know." I said it with conviction, finally finding my voice and recapturing it from the lost alleyway of the worst day of my life. The boy regained consciousness as the ambulance arrived. The islands entire medical staff, represented by the two men in polo shirts and faded khaki shorts, carried the scared boy away on a stretcher as a precaution. Walden delivered the vague details. I never knew the boy's name.

I would board the ferry in forty minutes leaving the island and all its faces behind. Walden and I stood on the beach staring into our relationship as the emptiness of the morning altered, and people began meandering along Main Street. Cars lined up in the ferry station lot while the two of us searched for words. My heart settled when I listened to the velvet sounds of the ocean and thought of water droplets climbing, knowing they would eventually make it. After all, I had.

"I guess you've saved another life." His eyes were fixed on me in a manner forcing me to understand.

"I almost did it without you this time."

"You would have done it without me either time." There were no ends to what I owed this man for his altruistic words. "However tragedy attacks you for the rest of your life, it will never control you again." He looked past me nodding toward the endless horizon. "You'll just go on." He waved his arm out over his stare implying he created the scene himself for us to enjoy. I don't know if that would have surprised me.

The professor made a strange entrance into my life in the proceeding days, and now he would exit with distressing permanence. I knew then on that small beach I would never hear another omniscient lecture again and I reached for the right words to express powerful appreciation for my mentor. I could not find those words, but I never doubted that he knew what I intended. I possess that certainty because of what he said just before we turned and walked away from each other.

"Just take one step at a time, brother." And then he turned away. Naturally, the last word, filled with life and hope, remains fixed in my memory. Walden accompanied me through the toughest time in my life as I navigated each step and prepared to exist alone. The last person who called me brother was Walter Roberts.

I boarded the ferry buried in abstract thoughts of all the changes I underwent in so little time, and the new experiences that reshaped me. Still confused, I felt stable and ready to move onward. Untethered, I stood by the ship's rail, as a salute to the tragedies we overcome, and looked toward the island I left behind. Richard Smith slept somewhere on that island and he would never be my father again. Near O'Mally's entrance in the distance, two figures stood motionless among the scrambling tourists. The statuesque, slender, dark figure with an unmistakable, graying beard smiled at the most beautiful woman I ever held, while my ferry moved out of the harbor. I was not surprised to see her with Walden, I was simply grateful for the last infinite picture of her that remains etched in my mind. Her shoulder seemed to flinch in a motion that could have become a wave, but her arm never moved. My eyes pierced her entire being, while I remembered the last three words she left for me: *With love, Megan.* The growing distance outlasted my vision as they finally blended with the crowd, and soon they were gone, forever.

Epilogue
Brotherhood

An elderly woman cried in rhythmic sounds of loneliness as she placed flowers on the grave of her husband. I wondered about her regrets as I walked cautiously between headstones. Thinking of her enabled me to suppress my own mortal fears and control my own regrets. My pulse slowed as I finally stared into the deep gray and read the words I avoided for too long.

Walter Roberts
Born: July 28th 1975
Died: June 13th 1994
WE BELIEVED IN YOU

"I'm not really sure what I'm supposed to say." Then I said everything, and for my own sanity I spoke aloud. "I miss you brother... and I'm sorry. I'm sorry I didn't answer you. I'm sorry I wasn't at the funeral. I just... it was hard. I met some people who helped me though. Not doctors or anything like that, just ordinary people. Well sort of." I stood in the cemetery for a few hours and continued speaking of times and mistakes to the memory of my deceased brother. I may have been the only one listening to my incomprehensible ramblings and incoherent emotions, but I'll always believe Walter heard me too.

It is strange that people never forget the hardest times in their lives. I've forgotten birthdays, ball games, friends, dreams, and oceans, but I'll never forget the day my best friend died in my arms, and I'll never forget three weeks of a summer which followed that day. The summer of new experiences, the summer of searching for, and never attaining forgiveness, the summer of conversations on a jagged wall where water climbed. The summer I left my father and I returned to my mother. The summer of calamari was the summer I found the courage to speak to my brother again. Walden was right when he said tragedy strikes us all. I now understand that we differ only in how we deal with it.

I walked out of the cemetery crowded with tragedies, thinking fondly of Walter Roberts, the best friend I've ever had, who taught me about brotherhood, not as a birthright, but as a huge commitment in life transcending blood lines. I'll never know if my brother forgave me when he closed his eyes for the last time, but on the toughest days I tell myself he did. I will only know that I loved and believed in him with all my strength, and I lost him, just before I rediscovered myself, in the safest and most dangerous summer of my life. While some of our memories have faded, slipping through my mind, despite a strong grip, I know that our brotherhood will last forever. Walter was right all along. People have to be saved one at a time.

Printed in the United States
32647LVS00001B/106-108

9 781420 822663